BLOOD DON'T LIE

A Novel

AARON LEVY

*In memory of Jeffery Fitzgerald
my old friend*

*For my parents,
Thelma and Jay Levy
who always did their best for our family
and their best was more than enough. . .
even when I didn't know it*

Blood Don't Lie

Because no battle is ever won he said. They are not even fought. The field only reveals to man his own folly and despair, and victory is an illusion of philosophers and fools.
–William Faulkner, ***The Sound and the Fury***

Cody: *Watch blood. Blood is a sign.*
–Steven Dietz, the play ***Trust***

CHAPTER ONE

Today, I'm a man.

And soon Sara Rothman will know it.

She wears a dress the color of a banana that straps over her shoulders, and high heels. Last year Sara Rothman actually invited me to her bat mitzvah and I almost asked her to dance, but, but. . .then I didn't.

"Today, Mr. Larry Ratner is a man," Rabbi Newman announces, ending the service part. My mom is crying, no bones about it, her makeup all over the place. My dad smiles and gives me a fist as our eyes meet that says, "We did it. We won the game."

Before I left the house today, I made a promise to my dog, Snowball, that as soon as my bar mitzvah party starts, I will ask Sara Rothman to dance.

She almost wasn't invited. My mom kept nagging me to give her a list of my friends for the kids-my-age table, you know, for the party. If we invite them in a timely fashion, she said, *maybe* they won't go waterskiing instead. Since moving to Cherry Hill, New Jersey, I've discovered all the kids-my-age show up to school on Mondays with ski goggle tans around their eye sockets from long weekends on giant boats. That's just true.

My mom finally gave me an ultimatum: either I give her a list of friends by the end of the day, or she takes matters into her own hands. So, I gave her a piece of paper with my older sister Marna's name on it, a guy from the old neighborhood who's actually dead, and Snowball. Oh, and Kevin. Who is Catholic. Pretty much a signed confession saying I have no friends in Cherry Hill. She looked at my list and said, "I guess you made your decision, Buster." Nothing good ever happens after my mom calls me "Buster." She got a contact list of everyone in my Hebrew School class, and she invited *all* of them.

My cousins and a handful of kids-my-age start filling in around me to take the kids-my-age picture. And Kevin. He sticks out like a deformed kosher pickle in this crowd because he's taller than all of the Jewish kids-my-age, and has stacked at least a dozen yarmulkes on his forehead.

"Big kids in the back, short kids in the front," the photographer announces. "That means Larry, you're right in front, kiddo."

I wouldn't mind starting a club, like an after-school club, for short people. It's something I can never get away from; even today, the day I become a man. As I watch the kids-my-age line up: I'm shorter than every one of them, even the girls.

I can see me at the Short Persons' Meeting:
ME: "Hi, I'm Larry, and I'm short."
EVERYONE: "Hello, Larry." Lots of short voices.

Except, what happens if I'm the shortest person in the short person's club?

There could be a club for girls with flat chests too. I sat next to Sara Rothman in English class this whole year, I guess because her last name is Rothman and mine is Ratner. Devon Sunther and Robert Bullock are all over her with small boobs jokes. When they really tease her bad, she only says, "You guys," like it doesn't bother her, and just gives this huge sigh with her bottom lip that blows her bangs up. But, it has to. I swear.

That's partly why Sara and I would go good together. In fact she's part of my twelve-step rehabilitation program to cure my shortness disease once and forever, except my program only has three steps so far: Dance with Sara Rothman tonight and forever, ah, you know, sort of; make the Beck Jr. High basketball team, and become real friends with Kevin. So. . .here goes.

Off with the jacket and the stupid vest thing. I look at the deejay. He gives me the thumbs up. It's on.

I strut across the party hall, which is decorated in blue and white balloons and streamers, a pure Israel theme. My mom did ask me what theme I wanted for my party, and I told her, Dr. J – Julius Erving, only the best Philadelphia 76er's basketball player of all time. He's still epic. He was Michael Jordan before there ever was a Michael Jordan. And Lebron James used to wear number 6 in honor of Dr. J. Serious. Well, I wanted to honor Dr. J too. . .at my bar mitzvah. I don't think my idea was Jewish enough because my mom chose Israel as a theme instead, with each table labeled a different Israeli city. But she did put blue and white cardboard basketballs in the center of every table.

I march past Tel Aviv and Jerusalem, to Beer-Sheva, right up to Sara Rothman, and tap her on her shoulder. This is one of those times when my brain is saying one thing and my body is doing something totally different.

"You wanna dance?" my body is asking.

Sara Rothman smiles because that's just what she does. "Sure."

I hope this doesn't get me more heat than I already get, but I'm not really a chest man. I mean if I got to second base with a girl, I wouldn't mind it. I'm guessing it'd be a good place to be. I'm only saying that if you don't think Sara Rothman is hot just because she might have a flat chest, then I don't know what you're looking at.

I'm concentrating on where my feet go, making sure I *to* when she *fros*, when she asks, "So what's it like?"

"What?"

Daylight by Maroon 5 is playing. I hate this song. They play it at the roller rink and people skate backwards to it.

"Being a man and all," she says, smiling like she's embarrassed to say I'm a man. Which is cool. I just wish there was a better song playing.

"What?" I say *what* to buy myself some more time so I can think of something really cool to say which comes out as, "Oh. Same. Like, same."

"We're dancing though," she says, and that's the truth.

"Hey, I'm even thinkin' about a fast one."

"Well I couldn't say no. I mean, this being *your* day and all."

"Oh, well, it's okay if you don't want to—I can ask my mom or somethin'—"

"I'm just kidding, you goofball." Sara punches me on the sleeve. I'm really thinking that maybe I should turn her a little. She probably thinks I can't dance because I haven't turned her and all we're really doing is rocking from side to side—"Actually, I'm honored you picked me first," she says before I can navigate the move.

"Even though you're still taller than me?" I ask, trying to sound like I'm making a joke. "Dang, if I was gonna become a man, you'd think I would have at least grown like an inch or something last night." I can't believe I just said that.

Sara Rothman laughs because that's the kind of girl she is. She knows it's a joke even if it isn't funny. Then she does something that is either awesome or pathetic; she takes off her shoes and I'm almost seeing her eye to eye now. It's scary how amazing her eyes are. Blue. That's all. The earth is blue too and that's no mistake. Sara Rothman blows her bangs back with her bottom lip and says, "There. Perfect. High heels should be against the law, you know? I hate 'em."

This is the first time I'm aware of where I am: On the dance floor with *people*. I check to see if they are looking at me. My sister, Marna, is dancing with my dad, standing on top of his shoes. Even though she's almost 16, she looks like she's only 6, dancing on his toes. Kevin is boogying with my grandma, laughing all crazy as he dips her. A grandma could pop a hip out or snap an ankle doing that.

"This is a dumb song," I say. I want her to talk.

"Yeah, it's lame but I kinda like it. The words. Not the singing. Or the music. And I'm only a little taller than you anyways, Larry." Then with one lighting quick move, she closes her eyes and makes me spin her. I spin her again and it's contagious this spinning and maybe I'm really good at dancing if dancing is just spinning. We're both laughing and breathing and when we stop spinning, Sara's attention is suddenly caught by what's going on near the bar.

"What?" I ask.

"Conceited," Sara says. "Robert Bullock thinks he's all that." We look at Robert Bullock and Devon Sunther and Toby Shaffren because they are stealing a bottle of champagne from behind the bar and wrapping Robert's suit jacket around it as if they've been doing this kind of heist for years. "He's just tall," she says, staring at him. "That's all he is - just, just a tall boy." For the first time during our dance she seems to fade off to another place besides being here with me. Seriously.

"My friend Kevin is tall too," I say.

"Hmm?" she asks. She smiles. She is on another planet. A very tall planet. When she finally comes back to earth, she looks over my head and says, "So how does it feel to be a man, Larry? You never said."

I shrug. "I mean, I'm still gonna have Captain Crunch with chocolate milk for breakfast if that's what you mean."

She laughs for a second. She's still looking all over the place. "I don't even eat breakfast, never have. My dad lets me drink the coffee he makes. I used to hate coffee, you know? But now I love it. And then I didn't eat lunch today 'cause I put my dress on before lunch time and I didn't want to spill on it which is weird 'cause this will be the last time I ever wear it."

"Why?" Sometimes Sara talks all fast and doesn't even stop to breathe. It's great.

"I'm not taking it with me. Too big and bulky."

"With you?"

"C'mon, Larry, you know I'm moving. I've only said it like a million times. . . Or maybe I didn't."

My heart is suddenly full of sand. "Oh," I mutter.

"Yeah, to Israel. Did I ever tell you my dad's from there?"

I nod, as if I know, even though I don't know jack. The only thing I can hear right now is how she's moving away. Forever. She should not be doing this to a person on his bar mitzvah! That's against Jewish law, right?

She tells me her whole family is moving to Beer-Sheva, a city about 20 miles from the Gaza strip, where Israelis and Palestinians are fighting over a tiny strip of land the size of like two Washington DCs. Her dad is still an officer in the Israeli Air Force and has been called back for duty because, and I swear Sara talks like this, "terrorist activity is heating up again." So her home in Beer-Sheva actually has a bomb shelter next to the mailbox, because sometimes, often, rockets will be launched from the other side of the wall, and rocket alarms go off, telling everyone to take cover in their bomb shelters. Sara tells me all of this!

Plus, if Sara Rothman lives in Israel for the rest of her life, after high school she'll have to join the Israeli army. We learned that in Hebrew School, how you don't go to college right away; everyone has to serve in the military for at least two years right after high school. I can't even imagine, Sara Rothman, the girl who drew kittens with big eyeballs, and doodled hearts with arms and legs on her English folder, the girl whose hair always smells like some kind of tropical drink, the only girl I ever really wanted to talk to, the girl I finally asked to dance with me; she's going to learn how to shoot a rifle.

"But you'll write me, right?" she asks. "My new address is on the Hebrew school list. Or Facebook?"

I nod, but feel like all the helium in every balloon in the room is now in my head. And I never wanted a lame song to never end so badly. But then it does.

Sara Rothman leans in and kisses me on the cheek and I swear this part is really happening. She pulls away, holding my neck and staring me in my eyes so intensely that it's scary. She says, "I'm going to make you a memory wax museum by pouring candle wax into one of those glasses that we'll steal—ah, take—I mean borrow, off a table and then all *your friends* will present it to you at the end of your bar mitzvah party and you'll feel special and you'll remember me forever every time you look at it."

She glows. If it were all the way dark in here, she'd be the only thing to see.

I don't know what to say so I just say, "Thanks for dancing with me. The song was lame and all, but. . ."

"Yeah the song was lame," she agrees. She bends down to put on her shoes, and holds onto my sleeve for balance.

If I move, she'll fall. Shoe-straps and all, she finally stands, now looking down at me. "I like the words though."

I'm stuck. Stuck right here. People start to swarm the dance floor because the lights change and the music is fast again. . .and all I can think about is the bathroom. After my bar mitzvah service and right before this party, I got sick. Ah. . .from both ends.

Because I hate public speaking. No. I hate public *being*. Anything that makes an entire room look only at me, to see how TALL I'm not, I hate. So, I don't remember doing any of the actual Hebrew-chanting-becoming-a-man part. I swear. To God. I don't.

What I do remember is after I got sick and I was sitting on the temple toilet, a holy throne, literally, recovering, I heard three kids-my-age enter the bathroom.

I just sat there, not making a peep, and listened. Peeing was happening.

"Do you even know whose bar mitzvah this is?" The first one said.

"Um," the second one said.

"Nope," the third one said.

"I think it's that short kid," the first one said. "But I don't know him."

"Who?" the second one said, apparently zipping up. "That really short dude?"

"I don't know him. My mom said I should go. Free food. Tunes. Party. So. . ."

"The short kid?" the third one asked. "No way. He looks like he's third grade."

Nobody answered. So maybe they were nodding.

"Who cares?" the first one says. "I'm on a serious jungle expedition assignment to locate the mosquito bites on one beautiful Sara Rothman. All over that."

Re-zipping happened. Flushing did not happen. Washing hands did not happen.

"Let's go suck down all the helium in this motha'," the second one said.

They left. I did flush. I did wash my hands. That all happened.

I realize it right now; the first kid from the bathroom was Robert Bullock.

"Hey, wait!" I yell after Sara, too loud. People are looking at me. I'm the bar mitzvah Boy and when the bar mitzvah boy says to wait, people listen. I smile, but I don't move. Because I'm stuck. I smile at my mom to tell her it's okay, keep dancing.

Sara is so cool, she just comes right back over to me. "Hmm?" She blows her bangs out of her face with her lip-balmed bottom lip. Watermelon.

I wait. Too long. She looks at my face, moves closer, then softly asks, "What?"

I lean into her and get up on my toes. "My friends here. . .are not my friends." I say to her ear in a whisper; the kind of whisper that secrets come in. I don't know why I'm saying this to her, but I know I'm saying it, and making sure she is hearing it. "My friends here are *not* my friends." Again I say it. It's weird, because it makes me sort of smile when I say it, all embarrassed, staring dead into her eyes until I can't anymore. "So, so you can't just move away, to the other side of the planet. Okay? Just. . . don't."

Devon Sunther and Toby Shaffren and Robert Bullock are going around to all the tables, taking the balloons – the blue and white ones my mom picked out – and sucking the helium out of them. Robert Bullock just laughs like he's too cool to put his own mouth on a balloon but not too cool to watch them do it. They suck down the helium, swallow all of the Israel in the room, and play the sucker punch game, punching each other in the arm as hard as they can from just a pinky space away and say, "Ouch, that's smarts," in their tiny Smurf-helium voices. All the kids-my-age laugh.

Sara Rothman has been staring at me the whole time. She can stare in your eyes and never flinch. Then she's on me like she's going to give me a giant hug, but instead gets right up to my ear and says, "Larry, memory wax museums never lie. Never ever."

And she's gone. I can still smell watermelon like it's under my fingernails.

I'm just stuck.

Last year I sat right next to Sara Rothman for 180 days and I talked to her more during one dance tonight than I had the entire year. The thing is, I had 180 days to do all of this and I never did.

Now, I watch Sara gather her girlfriends and steal a big glass off the Tel Aviv table. . .and disappear. Poof. They are going to make me something. ME. To honor ME at my party. How amazing is that?

I've never been so happy and so sad all at the same time.

Chapter Two

My mom assigns me to a table with all my friends who are not my friends. I'm at the kids-my-age table, also labeled The Wailing Wall. Oddly enough, I'm sitting between my sister and nobody, an empty chair reserved for Jackson McCaffery who couldn't make it. Jack was my best friend from the old neighborhood after everybody else left, before we moved to Cherry Hill. And even though I knew Jack wasn't coming, I asked my mom if we could save a spot for him anyways and she said, "That's a great idea, Larry. It's the right thing to do."

When I get to the table after dancing with Sara, Kevin's leaning all over my sister. "C'mon," he pleads with Marna. "I won't spin ya or dip ya or nothin'."

"Kevin," Marna says. "Right now, you're just creeping me out."

"There he is!" Kevin twirls around and then takes a swig of Jackson McCaffery's drink.

"Tell your friend to stop drinking Jack McCaffery's iced tea," my sister says.

"What? Dude's not even here," Kevin says, gulping down the rest of Jack's glass.

"Kevin," I say, and I mean it. "Don't drink Jack's iced tea, man. Just don't."

"Now fill it back up," Marna huffs and plops the pitcher of iced tea down in front of Kevin, who does what he's told.

While he pours, he whispers to me, "Dude, I gotta dance with your sister."

I look at Kevin drooling over Marna. He's weird but interesting, and he doesn't go skiing on the weekends, probably because he's too poor. Like me.

We both turn to the dance floor when we hear the music stop, and see a bunch of the kids-my-age emerge from nowhere and take over the stage.

"Uup, that's me," Kevin says as he jumps from his chair to the stage. They all swarm around the microphone to present me with my memory wax museum; which is just a giant glass that Sara's friends stole off a table and filled with all this stuff from my bar mitzvah. Then they melt candle wax in and all over the glass so it stays stuck in time, like a memory. That's the idea anyway. There's a ripped-up napkin with "Larry Ratner" printed on it, a part of a plate, three popped balloons, a slice of a flower, a chewed piece of gum, somebody's Chap stick, a barrette, a pile of what looks like a collection of boogers, a champagne cork, and some melted M&Ms from the dessert bar.

Sara gives it to Kevin and Kevin swipes the microphone. "I just wanna say that you folks sure know how to throw a party." All the kids-my-age and the whole crowd cheer. Then Kevin gets back on the microphone. "Larry, man, we made this for you. We almost lit this whole place on fire doin' it, but this is so you'll remember this day the rest of your life. Come take it, my brother."

And I do.

Back at the table, I grab Jack's straw and poke it through a thin layer of the wax at the top. If he were here, he'd have added something way more original, like a slice of cock-roach or a Risk game piece, but his straw will have to do.

Everyone wants me to dance with my mom. I do that too.

"So?" she says, as we awkwardly sway to some Barbara Streisand song she picked just for this moment. Great. "That was nice of your friends."

I look down. "C'mon, Mom, they're not really my friends."

Without skipping a beat, she says, "Remember, friends come and go," smiling like she's on the Red Carpet. "It's your blood—family—that you can always count on."

I want to tell her thank you; that this is the greatest party ever, but then I see Robert Bullock dancing with Sara Rothman. She's got her shoes on. They see eye to eye and it kills me. If I had her as my girlfriend it would automati-cally fix everything. I wouldn't be the shortest person at my school anymore, no way. Robert Bullock dips Sara and she screams as he swoops her back to her feet, loving it. She doesn't know that it's killing me on my special day. The day I became a man. It's not her fault. . .but she can't stop laugh-ing in his tall arms.

It's dark by the time we drag all of the presents and leftovers out to the car, but the moon is big and lights up the empty parking lot. It's sad to walk across the blacktop because it means I have to go back to being plain 'ole me tomorrow. And that Sara Rothman is still moving to Israel. My father puts a bunch of presents down and then sets my memory wax museum on the roof of the car as he finds his keys. My mom tells him to hurry and put the air conditioning on because it's still hot out at night in June. He turns the car on and I help him load up all the rest of the presents and leftover food.

He drives away, forgetting the memory wax museum is still up there on the car roof. And when it finally crashes in the street, my mom says, alarmingly, "What was that?" And then she turns off the radio and tells my dad to roll up his window. She's cold now. I will miss the wind in the back seat.

CHAPTER THREE

I t's the morning after I became a man, Sunday, the worst day to do a paper route because the paper itself is humongous and you have to put a million inserts in it. Yes, there are still people in America who want a physical newspaper delivered to their doorstep, and I'm the person that delivers it at the crack of dawn. I should have quit yesterday. I even promised Snowball that as soon as we got home from my bar mitzvah, I would inform my parents of this decision. . . but then I didn't.

A real man would have.

Part of it is my parents are all stressed out about money lately. I mean they are not doctors or lawyers like most parents in this neighborhood; my dad is a fourth grade teacher and my mom is a secretary in an elementary school office. And last year the Philadelphia School District went on strike so they didn't get paid for three months. My dad said they're supposed go on strike again this year. . . for even longer.

We moved from a townhouse in Bucks County to a new, what feels like a mansion, in Cherry Hill, New Jersey, so that we'd be in a better school district. There's actually a laundry shoot upstairs where your clothes get to take a giant sliding board ride down to the laundry room, that's how big this house is. One day Marna tried to stuff me in there, you know, just to see if I fit. And, well, I did.

Snowball, however, did not seem to like the new house. The day we moved in, he peed on the new carpet outside the hall bathroom on the first floor. And on the outside of my bedroom door, Marna's too, and a nice yellow puddle in the middle of the kitchen.

If you ask me, which they didn't, it's better to attend a crappy school in a crappy district than live in Cherry Hill and be all stressed out about money all of the time. Plus, I don't see what's so great about these schools, not one bit. Meanwhile, they said I had to get a job, which is this stupid paper route.

One of my routes is to serve the Regency Towers Apartment Building, and when I get to the lobby, I can't believe it, but Kevin is talking to the doorman. Seriously.

"Hey, man, what are you doing here?" I ask.

"Help. I'm all about the help," he says and directs me inside the building away from the doorman. "Really, I just want to go up to the roof like you said."

I forgot I told Kevin that sometimes I hang out on the roof of the Regency Towers Apartments because you can see all of New Jersey from up there. That's why I try to do the Towers last on my route so I can catch the sunrise. I'm not all into sunrises or flowers like you see on TV, but I kind of dig catching the sunrise up there, 'cause it feels like the sun jumps right off your shoulders when it finally comes all the way up. It's a great place to think and it's a great place to not think at all.

We sit on the edge and spit. There's nobody below, but it's kind of cool to think how you could really do some damage to people if you hit them square with some spit 28 floors up. Maybe even blind them if they suddenly look up at the same time a wad traveling 100 mph lands in their eye. That's some scary spit!

"So you and Sara Rothman?" Kevin says. "Not bad. She's a little vacant in the ta-ta department, but cute. But you're a munchkin too, so, yeah, it fits."

That's the other thing I hate about Cherry Hill. In my old neighborhood, I was short, but it's like I never really knew it. We all grew up together, so none of my friends really paid attention to how tall or short somebody was. Even Jack used to say, "Larry, you're not short. Stop getting your hair cut and you'll be fine." Then he'd pet my fro.

But here? My smallness is the biggest thing anyone ever talks about. Billboard big. So usually, I just ignore comments like what Kevin just said. Try to anyway.

"She's moving," I say. "To Israel. So. Yeah."

I don't feel like talking about it either; instead I just let my legs dangle over the edge, and spit. There's no railing up here, so if you scoot your butt forward just two feet, you'd be nose-diving off the roof to your death. When I look over or even think about it, I feel the electricity squirreling in my gut. It's a pretty awesome and overwhelming feeling.

"One day, we have to bring something huge up here, and let 'er rip," Kevin says.

We spit.

"Like what? A piano?"

"Nah, man. Bigger than that."

We spit.

It feels good to sit and spit up here with Kevin. I mean, I'm not sure where the point is when you go from knowing somebody to being their actual friend. I first met Kevin playing pick-up hoops at the elementary school by my house. A few times we were on the same team, and since I'm quick and can dribble, the bigger dudes usually let me handle the ball, and Kevin liked that I would pass it to him down low where he could do something with it. After he'd make a basket, he'd high-five me as we'd head back to the defensive end, and he'd say, "That's what I'm talkin' 'bout." I like that – I'd rather get 20 "that's what I'm talkin' bouts" than score 20 points any day.

But that doesn't mean we're blood brothers like me and Jack McCaffery and everyone from the old neighborhood. I haven't made any friends like that since we moved here. Not sure why. I mean I don't want to be pushy or needy about being friends with someone. That gets all weird, you know, like you're trying too hard for something that should just be natural. And I never had to do that in the old neighborhood. Just went outside, up to the cul-de-sac, and all my friends were there. It's just different here. But sometimes it seems like Kevin could be one. I don't know. Maybe if he had to introduce me to somebody and he said, "And this is my *friend*, Larry," I'd know what's up. God, now I sound like a girl almost.

"That was a great party." Kevin spits. "And your sister is HOT. Sorry I have to say that."

"It's okay." Even though it's not. I don't like Kevin slobbering over Marna. Just feels dirty or something.

"Don't tell her I said that," he says. "But you could put a good word in for me, you know, like sneak me into a conversation."

"What?" The electricity in my stomach makes me feel kind of sick now. I don't like it anymore.

"I'm just messin' with you, man. C'mon now."

Sometimes I wish Marna wasn't pretty.

We spit. From our throats this time, with phlegm. Big loogies. The sun is all the way up now, and we watched it happen. I'm not going to sit and talk about sunrises with Kevin, just not. We stand up and smack the roof dirt off our pants. Kevin stares out in the sky, and says, "Some day we'll come up here when it really matters. . .toss down something substantial, you feel me?"

I nod because I believe him. . .or at least I want to.

CHAPTER FOUR

Sara Rothman goes to Israel tomorrow. I go to Zigglersfield, Pennsylvania tomorrow, to sleep-away camp. So in the midst of packing, my mom announces, "We're going to the MAAAAAALL," to get me jeans that fit. It's not a choice. We're going to the Cherry Hill Mall, my mother's favorite place. I hate it. Marna hates it too, even though she's a girl and is supposed to love shopping.

See, we never just go to the mall, buy me a pair of jeans and leave. "Well, I don't know what size you are," my mom always says. "I'm not making a million trips." And I just think, why not? It's your favorite place to be in America.

If my dad were allowed to, he would hate the mall too. He just drives, holds bags of new clothes, and gives opinions about whether things fit. Typically, my mom will take the opposite of his advice. When we try on shoes, his job is to see where our big toes come to. He seems happy with this job.

The glass doors of the department store open and there are racks staring me in the face that are totally unrelated to what I was told our mall purpose is.

"Clearance," my mom says like a zombie to an incoming rack of clothes. "Just one second."

"And she's gone," my dad says. "Who knew there'd be a sale today? How strange." Even though my dad would hate the mall if he were allowed to, he still always makes jokes.

"I'm so bored," Marna says. "C'mon, Larry, let's go sit on a bench and watch time specifically disappear."

"I don't want to watch time disappear," I say.

"It's good for your coordination, Boy," my dad says.

Marna yanks my arm, pulling me to a bench away from the forest of racks. I see somebody I know come in the front door. Robert Bullock. He's with his mom and his mom is tall and I'll bet his dad has to duck just to get into a room or a car. My parents are the same size - short.

Robert sees me because he and his mom walk right past us. He nods. Of course, too, he looks Marna up and down.

"Mom, this is Larry," he says. "That's the bar mitzvah you made me to go to Saturday."

The one where he stole a bottle of champagne, I want to say. The one you sent him to, but neither of you knew whose bar mitzvah it actually was, I want to say. His mom looks down at me, surprised. "Oh. Yes. Hi, Larry, nice to meet you."

I was already irritated because I'm in the mall, and before Robert can go follow his mom to the racks of tall-people clothes, I pipe up:

"So, you going out for basketball this year?"

Robert just nods and says, "Of course. Coach wants me to."

"Right. Of course." I don't know what's wrong with me but when Robert turns to go I say, "Hey, I—I'm trying out for the team too. Nobody knows that yet." If I make the team, I'll be the shortest kid to ever make the Beck basketball team. But, like I said, I've got mad handles, maybe because I'm so low to the ground and people don't want to bend down to try and steal the ball. My shot is better too. My dad's even been coming outside lately to shoot with me and give me pointers. Last week, he showed me a spin move where I had to finish with my left hand. I couldn't do it at first, but he made me do it until I made 100 left-handed layups as he fed me the ball and counted, and kept saying, "yup," and "yes, sir!" and "that's the magic weapon," referring to my left hand. This might sound sad, but it was probably my favorite day on earth.

Robert just stares at me in disbelief, and gets me all nervous and when I get nervous I either don't talk or I talk too much. "So you—you better watch out."

That's when Robert snorts and then he laughs. . .and laughs. He's lookin' at Marna. "That's funny, Ratner," he says, still laughing and snorting. "Even Sara Rothman told me that about you – funny and small. No, it was *little*. That's what she said. A nice little guy, she said." He turns to find his mom and he just keeps laughing.

"Creepy," Marna says. "Staring at my boobs. Mr. Obvious. Mr. Creepy."

That's Marna's favorite word, "creepy," and it pretty much describes everything in her universe.

No way did Sara say that. No way. . . Wait. Did she?

"He's like two feet taller than you," Marna says. "Are you sure you're going into eighth grade and not like second?" First Sara. Now my sister.

I just ignore her. That's the only way to really bother Marna is to ignore her. I actually learned that trick from her.

My dad comes around the rack of women's socks and Marna quickly changes the subject. "C'mon, Larry. Let's go count to infinity or something."

This is something we do in the mall. She'll say one and then I'll say two and we'll go to infinity. In the Cherry Hill Mall, I swear, we almost got there before my mom finally decided it was time to go home.

CHAPTER FIVE

My parents have sent me and my sister to the same overnight camp for the last three years. Everyone who goes here is Jewish, but it's not like we sit around talking about God or rabbis or bagels all day. I just like this camp because the same kids come back every summer, so it feels like I have a ton of friends. Like the old neighborhood, but in the mountains. Plus people are supposed to grow in the summer, especially after they've been away at camp. That didn't happen to me last summer, but this summer I'm expecting to grow so much, my parents won't recognize me when they pick me up.

My best friend at camp is Danny Hellman, pretty much the toughest dude I've ever met. He's real skinny, but you can see every muscle on this guy, and he walks around shadowboxing all of the time. His dad used to be a pro boxer, but I've never heard of him. Danny boxes too, at a real boxing gym. He loves to talk about all the dudes he beats up back home in Philly though. I've never been in a fight. Not a real one anyway. He also likes to boast about how many girls he hooks up with. I believe him 100%.

You wouldn't think a guy like Danny Hellman would dig Dungeons & Dragons, but he really does, and we'd all play at night in our bunk for hours under a dome of flashlight glow. Danny said the stuff I had everyone go through when

I was Dungeon Master was better than any video game in the world. He said that. You wouldn't think a guy like Danny would be tight friends with a guy like me. . .but at camp, we totally are.

Every day after lunch is rest time, but we never play D&D then. It's gotta be dark and ominous to work right. Plus, we are required to write at least three letters a week during rest time, which doesn't sound like "rest time" at all.

I think I'm going to write one to Sara Rothman.

CHAPTER SIX

T he program was called *Escape from Germany.*
"It is 1939," Michael Levine, camp director, said two nights
ago introducing the evening program. "Germany. . .Nazi
Germany. And you. . .are *Jewish.* "

Meanwhile, this counselor, Bucky, who I'm pretty sure I
saw making out hard with my sister all summer, passed out
these yellow wristbands to all of us.

Basically, we had to form teams and pretend to be Jewish
families attempting to escape Nazi Germany while the counselors had to pretend to be Nazis sent to capture us, like a
Holocaust reenactment. I was on a team with Danny, Marcus,
this cute girl Jillian, and her annoying friend, Rachel. We
were told to go to different shopping points around camp
to pick up money, passports and various supplies before we
could get to a make-believe boat dock to escape the country.
Just like what Holocaust families had to do.

For me, it was more like Dungeons and Dragons meets
Jewish history, so it was sort of fun, but then everybody was
all serious, which made me feel all weird.

When our team finally arrived at the "boat dock," I saw
tons of other kids with puffy faces, like they'd been crying.
In fact, some were still crying, and lots of people were hugging each other. It was too weird. I didn't feel like hugging
anybody. It was all just a pretend game to me.

Apparently, I didn't feel like everyone else. And in three summers of going to Camp Arthur, it was the first time I can remember missing my mom and my dad. Like, suddenly I didn't fit in here; and for the first and only time, not because of my shortness disease.

And then, we are at breakfast on the very last day of camp. Danny is going on and on about hooking up with Danica Schaffrin during movie night last night. I keep looking at Danica over at the next table. She's my age, but today she looks a lot older.

Danny gets up to share his conquest with another table. Marcus comes back with his plate of waffles and takes Danny's seat.

"Hellman was sitting there," I say.

"So? He's not anymore."

Last week they were on the same team, celebrating after winning the inter-camp championship softball game. I remember watching Marcus and Danny at home plate, part of a full-team jumping bear hug. And two nights ago, we all escaped Germany together.

"Okay," I say. What do I care? I just know if Danny wants his seat back he'll probably get it back.

"Yo, Marcus, beat it, man," Danny says upon his return. "You're in my seat."

Marcus is at least two inches taller than Danny Hellman, and no slouch. He's chewing up his waffles, syrup dripping from his mouth. He says exactly what I thought he'd say, "I don't see your name on this seat."

Danny smiles, giving Marcus a chance to change his mind, "That's my seat, Marcus. You're in it. And you better get out of it. Now."

Marcus stands up and says, "Make me." And just like it was the next thing to say, Danny rears back and punches

Marcus square in the nose. I've seen fights before and there's usually some rolling around wrestling type thing that happens, maybe some punches which leads to some grabbing and then the fighters are on the ground until teachers come and pull them apart. But this one's different. One punch and Marcus falls directly backwards, his nose a bloody mess, barely breaking his fall to the cafeteria tile with his right arm. Danny just stands there with this wild look in his eyes. Two counselors jump in to break it up, but there's nothing to break up. It's already over, and all Danny says is, "Dude was in my seat."

Two nights ago Danny Hellman and Marcus were Jewish teammates escaping from the SS. We all wore the same yellow wristbands. This morning, though, Danny Hellman took another member of his tribe and laid him out cold on the cafeteria tile. I'm just sayin'.

Nothing else really happened at camp.

Except I miss Snowball like crazy. I hope, for his sake, he didn't pee in the house while I was gone.

And it's all over the news now, just like my dad told me: The Philadelphia School District strike will officially begin the first day of school. So my parents are officially unemployed.

Also, I wrote 14 letters to Sara Rothman during rest hours at camp.

I put her Beer-Sheva, Israel address and a special $2 stamp on each one.

I mailed exactly. . . zero.

And officially, I did not grow.

CHAPTER SEVEN

The bus stop is a place for zombies to gather and wait for this yellow tube of death to arrive. Another summer went by where everybody grew and I didn't. I won't be the smallest boy in the 8th grade; I'll be the smallest *person*. This is not an exaggeration; I'm not a midget, but I'm almost as short as one, barely sniffin' 4' 10". Maybe God forgot to make me grow because I was away at overnight camp and he couldn't find me.

My parents don't say anything directly to me, but I heard my mom say to my dad, "He's small. Little. Littler than the other kids, even the girls."

"Well, we can put him in the oven," my dad joked. I hope. "Cook him longer?"

My parents ended up getting me karate lessons for my birthday. Which is actually cool, and I start this week. Apparently, I'm on a special "scholarship" at the karate place until after the strike ends, so my mom said I'd better take full advantage and work hard.

I climb up the bus stairs and the driver grabs my arm. "The army is small but the army is proud," he says, winks, lets go, and goes back to reading the newspaper that's open on the steering wheel. What's weird is he looks like he's about 100 years old, but his whole body from what I can see – arms, legs, even his neck – is covered in tattoos. I don't want to stare at his old man inked skin, but his right shoulder is splattered with a bright green tattoo of Aquaman, who happens to be my favorite superhero.

"What army?" I ask softly, and find a seat in the exact middle of the bus.

We hear the static of the CB radio announcement gizmo over the bus speakers. And then it blasts that screech sound, like a cat slowly being flattened with a rolling pin, which makes all of us on the bus cover our ears and scream.

"First rule on my bus," the bus driver says, "is no screamin'." He has some kind of accent from another country. Not England or Australia, but I can still totally understand what he's saying. Maybe he's been in America a long time.

"The rules are simple. No hittin', pissin', gropin', fightin', poopin', standin', or screamin', or being mean ta each other on my bus. Keep ya clothes on ya bodies and ya hands in ya pockets and we'll get ya there and back with the greatest of ease."

He lets out a giant breath into the CB gizmo, and I'm telling you, we all could smell it. Like sardines or something. He keeps breathing old man breaths into the gizmo, and all you can see is his furry eyebrows and humungous eyeballs in the rear-view mirror; just half a face gasping for breath up there until he finally says, "Ya follow the rules real good. . .and on the first Monday of each week, I'll show you all one of my tattoos and tell ya what they mean. It'll be Mr. Cebulski's Tattoo Show-n-Tell Day. That's my name, don't wear it out. Call me Mr. C, but don't call me when I'm mergin' onto Kressen Road. Sit back, sit down, and sit up straight. Here we go." Click. CB off.

Everybody sits down and kind of looks around as the bus starts to roll. I can see his huge forearms lean on the big black steering wheel in the rear-view mirror as he turns us onto the road, but I can't make out all of his tattoos and what they are, just Aquaman. I want to though, like a sneak-a-peek. So when he stops and we are waiting in line to get off, I jump up to the front so I can get a better look, but just as soon as he opens the bus door, he also opens his newspaper, which covers his whole face and arms. I see stacks of newspapers covering the dashboard by the door lever. There must be three different newspapers on top of magazines. As I turn the corner to walk down the steps, I can see that at least one of them is not written in English. Looks like some kind of hieroglyphics.

CHAPTER EIGHT

It's the first day of school and I already hate all of my classes. My social studies teacher tells us that last year she sent 40 students to the principal's office. She doesn't want to surpass that number, she says, a school record, but she will if she has to. My English teacher, Mrs. Graham (aka Mrs. Grammar Tree) made us stand up and say what we did this past summer. I hate talking in front of the class, so I said, "camp," and then sat right back down. For our big final paper, we have to write an essay where we compare and contrast two things. It's worth over half our grade she says, and then she laughs out loud like essays are punch lines to jokes in her world.

My algebra teacher is Mr. Cunningham, who is also the 8th grade basketball coach. I remember him from last year when I used to stay after school and watch practices. He's this tall bald man with a basketball for a belly, who never smiles, and he only picks tall kids for his basketball team too. There's one kid less than six feet, but according to Kevin, he's the only kid on the team who can dunk. But like I said, I've been working on my game, and I'm sure they need another ball handler. I was planning on shooting 500 shots every day after school until winter tryouts, but then Mr. Cunningham announces that tryouts are in two weeks.

After class I approach Mr. Cunningham at his desk. It's full of round coffee stains. He's got his face in the sports section of the Philadelphia Inquirer before the kids have even left the room.

Without looking up, he says, "What can I do for you, son?" still reading like a whole article in the damn newspaper, like I'm not even right in front of him.

"I was planning—I'm planning to try out for the basketball team, but—"

He folds the paper and squints, fitting my small body into his big eyeballs.

"I was playing league ball this summer, sir." I don't know why I'm calling him "Sir," or why I'm lying. I never call anybody that, but I do seem to lie a lot. "A, ah, a tough league, up north, sir."

He looks back down at his newspaper while saying, "Tryouts are in two weeks. Cuts in three, but. . ." Mr. Cunningham laughs, which seems totally unnatural. Crooked jaw, coffee breath, yellow teeth, lousy laugh; I just want to leave.

"Look, son. You can come try out that first week, sure," Mr. Cunningham says. "But, you know?" He smiles, sort of waves his hand over me like I'm a new car and he's a supermodel on TV showing off my sleek, short frame. "You may be more suited for intramurals. I mean, this is a big-boy league. Not a t-ball-everybody-plays type deal. To be honest, I pretty much have my team. They've been playing for me all summer. But you can come try out that first week, sure."

"Thank you, Sir. I've been playing all summer too, Sir." Which is a total lie. I've been escaping from Germany and pretending to cry with Jillian Lipshultz, that's what I've been doing.

"You need a pass to your next class?" He pulls out a drawer that has a million passes to class and fills one out, all fast and sloppy like a doctor. Feels like Mr. Cunningham already just cut me, but I'm going to try out anyway. That's it.

CHAPTER NINE

The day gets worse in PE. There are four different PE teachers and they all look exactly the same. They all have mustaches; their hair parted to the same side, and those coach's pants pulled up to their belly buttons. But after my PE teacher, Mr. Stack, spends the better part of an hour talking about the dress code – how to dress out, how to behave in a locker room, what happens to you and your family if you dare to show up to PE without the proper dress – he starts to talk about what we are going to do during PE this year. I've always really liked PE because you play all the sports and then War Ball in between units. So PE never really bothered me. . .until now:

"Men," that's how PE teachers address you, maybe because they get to see you naked in their locker room. "This year is going to be a great year. A GREAT YEAR!" And PE teachers only have one volume level: loud, aka, coach-speak. "This year we'll be starting a new kind of unit. Can you say *new unit*, men?"

Does he want us to repeat the words *new unit?*

Like most PE teachers, Mr. Stack's teacher face goes completely red and his neck veins come out, huge blue snakes as he screams, "CAN YOU SAY *NEW UNIT*, MEN?!"

We all scream, "new unit!" because we're all afraid of his giant neck vein snakes.

"There it is!" He pauses, his veins settle, morphing back into his neck, and then he unleashes the bad news: "Square dancing." An evil smile crawls across Mr. Stack's face; his mustache is almost twinkling. "That's right, square dancing."

Wait, what? I can't believe what I'm hearing. Who would ever put dancing in a class where you're supposed to learn how to play sports? He tells us that square dancing is a new addition to the curriculum, whatever all that means.

"And, men, here's the good part. You don't square dance by yourselves. HECK NO! You dance with ladies!" What? "The lovely gals in Ms. Gimp's class."

Great. Now we've gotta pick out a girl and hope that she's halfway decent looking and that she wants you to pick her, and – that nobody picks her before you do or else. . .you're left with the girls nobody wants as their partners to choose from. I mean it's not like Sara Rothman goes to my school anymore. Seriously.

I hate square dancing. I hate dancing, period – I don't care what shape they make you do it in. Circle dancing or triangle dancing would suck too.

The bell rings. The first day of school is over. It's the worst day of my life. Clearly. Dancing. In PE. Blasphemy! I hate school.

Kevin almost tackles me on my way out to the bus, and I can't help thinking how lucky he is he can just walk home. "Can you believe we have to do square dancing?" he asks, holding me up until I have my footing. "I'm thinking about transferring schools to one that doesn't make you do lame things. Yeah."

"No doubt," I say. "Hey, man, I gotta go or I'll miss my bus."

"Alright. Then I won't tell you what I heard about you at lunch today."

"What? Me? What did you hear about me?"

"No, no, you have to catch the banana mobile. I understand."

"C'mon, man, I do or I'm stuck here. Just tell me real fast."

"Monica Johnson wants you to ask her to be your square dance partner."

I'm shocked. Monica and her friends all wear the same designer jeans (don't ask me the brand because I'd just say, Tight Brand, as in tight-tight, as in tight-just right-tight). She's got sparkly brown eyes that always seems like they're about to cry, even when she's laughing, and curly locks (what we Jews call "Jew hair"). In other words, Monica Johnson is really hot. And, as a bonus, only slightly taller than me, by the poof of her poofy hair.

"This is a good thing," Kevin says. "She thinks you're *cute*, and she's smokin' hot." A lot of people think I'm cute the way a puppy is cute. That's the way that's going to be. It doesn't usually mean they want to dance with me. Maybe touch my curly hair or pinch my dimples, and then on to a taller kid.

"Who told you that?"

"I thought you had to catch the bus?"

"C'mon. Who told you that?"

"If I tell ya my source, I have to kill ya." Kevin shrugs his shoulders, flashes that giant Kevin smile and disappears down the hall.

CHAPTER TEN

Monica Johnson thinks I'm cute. I walk up the steps of the bus. Monica Johnson thinks I'm cute. These are good thoughts to have on the bus. Monica Johnson thinks I'm cute. I just want to sit here, right in the middle of the bus, and think about Monica Johnson. Me and her dancing. . .in a square.

"Raaatner!"

It's Robert Bullock calling me from the stairs, by just my last name. He must be a future PE teacher because that's how they address everyone too. I'm sure Mr. Cunningham puts down his newspaper when Robert Bullock goes up to his desk. Anyway, note to self: don't sit near Robert Bullock.

But today *he* sits right next to *me*. It's the first chance that I've really looked at him since I saw him at the mall. He must've grown six inches this summer. I put my hands in my pocket and scoot all the way to the window.

"What are you doin' there with your hands, Ratner?"

"Nothing," turning my head to the window, away from him.

"What?" he says, tapping my shoulder. "Playin' pocket hockey?"

"No—"

"Hey Devon, check out Ratner here playin' pocket hockey."

Devon is in the seat across from us. Four other guys turn to look at me.

"That true, Ratner?" Devon's in on it now. They need a hall monitor for this bus, I swear. The bus driver looks in the rear view mirror. I see his eyes, but he doesn't see mine. And then back to the road.

"No," I say again, shrugging, scooting closer to the window.

"Well, see, he's right," says Bullock. "What really happened is that he wanted to play pocket hockey, but right now he's, you know, trying to find his stick, but you know, he's havin' trouble locating it. Everything is itty-bitty, like the rest of 'im. Maybe dig a little deeper there, Ratner."

Everybody's laughing. I am too. If you play along and act like it doesn't bother you, then usually punks like Robert Bullock move on to the next guy. I look out the window. My stop doesn't happen for three stops. An eternity.

"Hey, Ratner?" He's back on me. I hate how he says my last name all the time. "You hear about Sara Rothman?"

"She moved to Israel," I say, trying to sound uninterested.

"Can you believe that? I mean I'm Jewish, but I ain't *that* Jewish. I mean you gotta join the army when you get outta high school there. Man."

"She told me she wants to join the army," I say. Because she did.

"Guess what?" Robert asks me.

"No. It's okay," I say and look out the window.

He flicks my ear. "Guess what. Don't be rude, Ratner. Guess *what* when I say guess what. C'mon."

"Fine. What?" I turn to look at him.

"I got to third base with her," he tells me.

"What?" I say, louder and whinier than I wanted to. "With who?"

"Pay attention, Ratner. Sara. Rothman. Yeah, before she left, I hit that."

"You did not," I say, turning to look at him now.

"Yeah I went to second base and there was nothing there, so I just went straight to third."

Robert cracks up. Devon cracks up. I forget to crack up. Boob joke. Ha ha. Five other guys around us crack up. I'm not sure why this is devastating or why I even believe it. "You did not," I say involuntarily.

"Call her and ask her. Sorry, Ratner, I know you liked her. But a man's gotta take advantage of his opportunities. More than once too. Even at your bar mitzvah. . . Yeah, while you were playin' pocket hockey, I was hittin' that hard."

The bus stops. I'm stunned. I can't hide it and need to be hiding it.

"I didn't like her," I say. Lying. But I want that out there for the record.

"Don't lie, Ratner." He smiles big and evil.

"Yeah," Devon chimes in. "I thought Jews weren't supposed to lie."

I turn back to window. Just want to be home!

"She's in the army now anyway, Ratner," Robert says gathering his backpack.

He flicks my ear, this time too hard. Harder than I even think he meant to. It stings, "Uup, my stop." He stands over me like some kind of giant and says, "Hey, Ratner, you got something on your shirt."

He points at my shirt as I look down and then flicks my nose and laughs. "Gotcha. Oldest one in the book." Devon laughs too and so does everybody around me again. Robert gives Devon a high-five. He calls back as he is about to go down the bus stairs. "Gotcha, Ratner."

At home, I go directly to the basement, turn on the TV and put on the channel that plays old cartoons from like 20 or 40 years ago, I don't know, and watch *Super Friends, Justice League* until my mom calls us for dinner. I don't usually watch cartoons anymore, but when I did, I used to watch these old ones because those super heroes were better than the ones today. The old Super Friends is the Justice League that has Aquaman in it, just like the one on the bus driver's arm. There he is right now, swimming with killer whales. Whatever. I'm not even really watching it; I'm just zoning out, because if I think about Sara Rothman actually going to third base with Robert Bullock, at my bar mitzvah no less, I might have to take her giant army rifle and shoot myself.

CHAPTER ELEVEN

Sometimes my mom magically knows the exact day to make rigatoni with tons of cheese and meat sauce, aka my favorite meal. It's a mom mental-telepathy that kicks in while I'm at school when it's all lousy with square dancing and Robert Bullock, that tells her: red alert—rigatoni time.

I just want to eat and eat some more.

"Okay," my mom says when nobody's talking at the dinner table. "Either the first day of school was just loads of fun or my cooking is really delicious."

My mouth is overloaded with noodles.

"I'm not going to do debate team this year," Marna announces, and drops her fork to her plate so there's a *ding*. Last year, she was the youngest student to ever win a debate tournament or something like that. She's really good at arguing. Everybody in this family knows this. I wish I was as good with words as Marna, but I'm just not and never will be.

"Why?" My dad asks. "You did so well last year."

"You can't just quit, honey," my mom says. She doesn't believe in quitting anything. Years ago, she had to convince herself that quitting smoking was a good thing.

"Well, technically I wouldn't be quitting since the team is a year-to-year deal and I haven't started this year yet." See? That's why she's a good debater.

"Besides," Marna continues, "I don't really want to join a club whose sole objective is to argue on purpose. We can do that right here at home."

My parents laugh, so I think it's time for me to make my announcement.

"I'm going to try out for the basketball team this year," I say.

The whole table stops eating, except for Marna, who wasn't eating anyway.

"Oh," my mom says and looks down at her plate, kind of like Mr. Cunningham and his newspaper.

"Yeah, Lar?" my dad asks, puzzled. "When are tryouts?"

"Two weeks. Coach Cunningham says he's pretty much got his team. But. I don't know. I should probably try out. You know. Since there're tryouts and all."

"If he already has his team, why does he hold tryouts?" my mom asks.

"Because," I say, "it's like, I don't know, tryouts."

My dad leans back in his chair, hands folded over his belly, just sort of staring at me, with a look that's like, *okay, what are you up to, Mr. ?*

"It's the corrupt world of pre-prep-athletics," my sister says. "News at 11."

I drop my fork on my plate. *Ding.* "Fine, I won't try out."

"Whoa, whoa. Hold the boat." My dad always tries to make peace.

"I just thought it was something I could do," I say.

"You can," my dad finally says. He glares at my mom. "He can."

My mom looks at me as if I'm about to step into the jaws of a killer whale by accident. "Of course," she says, hardly moving her mouth, so God won't see her faking. Everybody goes back to eating. In silence. Except for Marna, who doesn't really eat food much anymore. She sort of pushes it around her plate.

It's my fault nobody's talking, so I say, "My bus driver has nine tattoos."

"Huh," my dad says and then gobbles a forkful of pasta.

"That's against Jewish law you know," my mom says.

"It is not," Marna says.

"Ah, hello?" My mom says this when she wants the floor. "Did you miss learning about the Holocaust in Hebrew School? Jews were branded with numbers on their wrists in the concentration camps? So now to honor those Jews who didn't have a choice whether to be branded or not, we do *not* desecrate our own bodies on purpose with permanent ink thank you very much."

"First of all," my sister says. It's on. Debate team competition right at our kitchen table, just like she predicted. "It wasn't just Jewish people who were branded with numbers on their wrists. And second of all, it's not a Jewish *law*. Nowhere in the Old Testament, or the New Testament for that matter, does God say, *thou shalt never paint Mickey Mouse on thou bicep.* C'mon."

"Well, okay," my mom says, somewhat defeated. "It's just wrong, symbolically, how about that?" And she gulps a forkful of rigatoni for emphasis.

My dad says, "Hey, Marna, you ever think about joining the debate team?"

"Hey Marna," my mom says. "Is this against Jewish law?" And then, I swear, my mom throws one pea and it bounces off of Marna's nose.

"Gross!" Marna screams. I laugh.

"Not kosher, young lady," my dad wags a finger at my mom, pretending to be a rabbi. "Not kosher at all."

We all laugh a little bit. Even Marna cracks a smile. The thought of starting a giant food fight occurs to me, but my mom's rigatoni is too good. It's definitely against Jewish law not to eat it.

CHAPTER TWELVE

My parents go to our open houses after dinner that night.

I find Marna in the dining room staring at the boxes of Girl Scout cookies piled to the ceiling. Truth be told, they are left over from Marna's troop's spring sale. Apparently our house is the secret headquarters for lost and lonely, yet-to-be-sold Girl Scout cookies.

"You want some?" Marna asks me.

"I don't have any money," I say.

"Look at how many boxes there are. Who's gonna know?" She leans forward and grabs a box of Chocolate Peanut Butter.

"But you're allergic to peanut butter," I warn her.

"It will be so worth it, Larry. You don't even know."

Marna is in a fantastic and weird mood. "I. . .I hate the peanut butter ones."

"So?" she says, in a high-pitched fairy tale voice. "Take what you want, sweet boy. You deserve a break today. Here, you like Thin Mints."

No, I *love* Thin Mints. Once the box is in my hands, I'm in a serious hypnotic trance and I don't think about the fact that we're stealing. I just open the box, rip the plastic wrap with my teeth, and chomp down. It's exactly what I need, what I deserve, after such a lousy day. In mid-chew, with chocolate and mint in my teeth, I say, "What if the Girl Scouts find out you skimmed from the top?"

"I'm not a Girl Scout anymore, Larry. . .I'm in love." Marna throws a whole peanut butter chocolate in her mouth, chewing and laughing. "And that's why we are gathered here tonight. 'Fank you," she says, spraying my shirt with peanut butter cookie fragments.

"Gross, stop," I say. "What—who. . .does Mom know?"

She swallows the cookie. "Slow down, kid." She likes to call me "kid" a lot. "I'm in *love* here. Okay? So just, okay? And don't look at me like that, like you don't know what being in love is, 'cause I happen to know you do, little brother. There are two of us in love here, eating illegal cookies tonight in the dining room, but only one of us is woMAN enough to admit it."

"I'm not in love—"

She picks up the box of Thin Mints and bonks me on the head with it. "I'm sorry," she says. "But a person that writes 40 million letters to one girl, doesn't send *any* of them? That's a little dude in love."

"What the hell—"

She raises the Thin Mint box, threatening to bonk me again. "Relax. I wasn't snooping. Mom told me to take your basket of laundry up to your room and there it was on top of your dresser, next to your prized Dr. J headband, the only item allowed to occupy the holy space on top of your dresser since you were 5 years old. So excuse me if a box full of letters to a girl in Israel suddenly stood out." She pops another whole cookie in her mouth and in mid chew, says, "It's okay. You're in 8th grade, you don't have to admit that you're in love."

"I'm not in love!!!!!!!" I scream, louder than I really want to.

"Okay, fine, you're not in love," she says all nonchalantly. "But if I were in love with a cute girl who lives in Israel, I wouldn't be scared to say it. I'd send those letters too. I'd be proud. Like I'm proud to say I'm in love with Bucky Hunt—"

"Bucky?!" I interrupt her and she nods. "From camp? Of course! I knew—."

"And no, Mom does not know," Marna says, a sly smirk taking over her face. "She doesn't know. And she doesn't know that I quit Girl Scouts either."

"You quit Girl Scouts too?! But you've still been going—"

"She *thinks* I've been going," she says as she pops another whole cookie in her mouth. "Lori picks me up and we go see Bucky and she hangs with Bucky's friend, Hector. All this stays zipped too or I'll hunt you down, little brother." And then Marna opens up her mouth to show me her chewed-up, half-digested cookie. I show her my mouthful too, and we're laughing, which Marna hasn't really done with me in, I don't know, years maybe it seems. But she's in love now, so. . .I'm not though. I'm not.

I swallow and wipe my mouth with my sleeve, and then it occurs to me, so I ask, "You're not going to bring him over to the house are you?"

"Oh no."

"Good."

"No. Nope. Uh-uh."

"Wouldn't be good," I say.

"Are you crazy? Plus, hello? He's 22 years old, so, yeah, not happenin'." She pops another cookie in her mouth and starts to laugh. She says, "Are you crazy?" again while she's laughing and little cookie parts are dribbling out of her mouth and even her nose. I start to crack up too.

Marna's starts acting even weirder, but I guess that's what happens when you're in love. She starts to fan herself with a napkin. "I'm so hot all of the sudden," she says, cracking up more. Like she's drunk – Girl Scout cookies make her tipsy. And then I see these red patches all over her neck and arms begin to erupt splotch by splotch – an alien shedding one entire skin and turning into something else, with brand new red, blotchy skin. It's really gross.

"Marna, oh my God! You're totally breaking out!"

"Yeah, really bad too," she laughs some more; a mad scientist. She sticks another cookie in her mouth before I can grab it from her.

"Stop! C'mon! You're all full of hives. What are you doin'?!"

"But they're so good. I can't help it." I've never seen her quite like this. Marna's crazy. She warns me again to keep all these secrets to myself and then she takes her blotchy hive-infested self back to her room and calls Bucky Hunt.

"Buck?" she sings and giggles. "Ah, like, I might be dying." Her door slams behind her and she is totally cracking up laughing.

My sister is in love. I am not. Besides, Monica Johnson thinks I'm cute too. So. . .

I go to the trash can and rip the green and yellow boxes into fingernail-sized shreds to destroy the evidence.

TATTOO SHOW-N-TELL #1
INSTALLMENT

*Y*eah, on this arm, up a bit, I've got a heart with my mom's name. . .MOM, in it. 'Cause I love my mom, God rest her soul. Okay then, sit back, sit down, and sit up straight. Here we go.

CHAPTER THIRTEEN

On the bus ride home, Robert Bullock sits wherever I sit. Sometimes if I sit where there's a cushion of people on either side of me, thinking there's no way he can sit near me, he switches seats with somebody by saying, "Hey, switch with me, dude," and the kid just moves.

Today I find a seat far away from Robert Bullock, in the middle of the bus.

He finds me.

I'm trying to ignore Robert Bullock after he flicks my ear, connecting only twice. The whole time, too, he is making fun of me because I'm going to try out for the basketball team, but whatever. He's really good at flicking me just hard enough so it hurts but not so hard that it hurts too much. So I try to act like we're just messing around today, like dudes do on the bus even if one of them (me!) never really wants to. That's the way I'm trying to play it. Control. Stay in control.

I just want to be home. On days when I don't have karate, I've been shooting 500 shots a day, getting ready for tryouts. Today is a karate day though, so in about an hour my mom will drive me to karate, and this bus ride will be a distant blip on the radar of the crappy things that happen today. Right now, though, I'm stuck.

Karate is not like the movies. It's hard. But I still like it. We do push-ups on our knuckles and if kids don't try or if they mouth off, the karate instructor, or sensei, who is a third-degree black belt, makes you get on your knuckles in push-up position and he whacks you on your butt with a bamboo stick. Serious.

Every other month you test for a higher belt and I'm almost ready to test for an orange belt, which is the first belt after white. Not that I talk to anybody at school anyway, but when I do, I don't really mention that I take karate. First off, I remember one kid last year told everybody that he was taking karate, next thing you know, everybody's picking fights with him. Second off, our sensei is always telling us the key to karate is to learn how to fight so that you never have to fight. What? I can't wrap my mind around that concept yet. It's like taking flying lessons and then only driving cars. He says stuff like, "Manage your anger. If you fight with anger, you lose control and become weak. When your opponent is angry, he loses self-control, and you have won." So if I don't get angry, I don't have to fight because I've already won the fight that I never got into in the first place? Maybe when I'm a green belt I'll understand it all better. All I do know is our sensei doesn't want us going around bragging that we take karate.

Flick. "Hey, Raaaaaatner," Robert says laughing. "Sara Rothman called me last night from Jerusalem. She wanted me to tell you to stop thinking about her or else I will have to kick your butt."

"Yeah, right," I say. I laugh. I think about controlling my anger. It's funny, I love sparring, but it doesn't mean I like fighting. In fact, to be honest, I quit fighting when I was in 5th grade because everyone grew and I didn't.

It takes more control to *not* hit someone while sparring, my sensei says. Control is everything. I mean in sparring you work on your kicks and punches and blocks, but you don't actually land any with full power. If you do by accident, that makes the sensei mad and you do 20 knuckle pushups.

"Devon, you hear this? Ratner doesn't think I can kick his butt." Robert screams this across the whole bus because Devon is in the way back.

"No, I never said that—"

Devon stands up and hollers, "Kick his butt, Robert! Do what you do!" Then Devon goes back to whatever he was doing.

Robert pats me on the back. "I like you, Ratner. You make me laugh. Ha. Ha. You think you can kick my butt. You and what army?"

"No army," I say and look out the window. I want to tell him that I'm taking karate, but I know I can't. That would be sort of like losing control, right? "Besides, Sara Rothman didn't tell you that anyways," I say to the window.

"So you're calling me a liar now? Ratner, you're lucky you're short. Like midget short. I never hit a kid with that kind of disability. Just not how I was raised," he says as he flicks my ear again.

If I make the basketball team, we'll be playing for the same team. Would he be flicking my ear then? Like instead of a high-five? Same religion, same team, same seat on the bus. He laughs. Is it funny or does he want me to know that he's just playing around? "Besides," he says, "you're the one who's lying."

"Yeah, right," I say.

"You said you could kick my butt. Now how is that not a lie?"

I don't want to answer him, so I don't. Plus it's so loud on the bus right now, like crazy-volume, so I'm pretending I didn't hear him.

The bus stops and Robert stands up to leave, thank God.

He brings his face down to mine really quick like he's going to deliver a massive head-butt, but instead he gets right up to my eyes so I can see his crazy look and says, "I'll tell Sara you say blah blah blah nothin'. 'Cause I talk to her *every day*," he says, punching every syllable in the word *every* and *day*.

Then he backs up to leave, finally, but right before he steps into the bus aisle, as he swings his backpack up over his shoulder, he flicks my ear. Hard. Way harder this time, to where my hand instinctively covers it, and I yell, "Ouch!!"

I didn't mean to yell anything. Especially not *ouch* – a real man doesn't say *ouch*, that's for sure. I didn't mean to say anything. I didn't mean to cover my ear or scrunch my face or especially make everyone on the bus. . .stop. And look. At me. It was insanely loud two minutes ago. Now all you can hear is the sound of feet that were shuffling down the aisle, no longer shuffling, and of course, the sound of quiet snickering at me. The sound of everyone's eyes on me.

The bus driver finally beeps his horn and says something like, "keep it movin'," I think, but my hand is still covering my ear because it really hurts. The truth is I want to cover both my ears, close my eyes, and just be home.

"See you tomorrow, Raaaaaatner." I can hear my name start from the stairs and echo out on the street.

I've never really thought about my name, but I'm starting not to like it.

And I hate his name.

I hate Robert Bullock.

CHAPTER FOURTEEN

At home I go right to the mirror and see my whole ear looks like it's on fire. When I first got home, I could hear Marna on the phone laughing all loud and fake and syrupy, so it scares the crap out of me when she shows up behind me in the mirror.

She takes in a huge breath when she sees my ear. "Oh my God! Oh my God, what happened to your ear?!"

"Nothing." I smack my hand over my ear, covering the swollen flick mark.

To the phone Marna says all loud and full of drama, "His whole ear is bright red—I don't know; I'm trying to find out. Hold on. Larry, what happened to your ear?!"

"Nothing. I. . .I fell."

"Buck, Buck, let me call you back. If you saw his—like, like a, like a big tomato exploded out of the top of it. This is—yes, yes, let me call you back," she says. Before she hangs up, a giant smile crawls across her face. "Don't call me that. I don't like that." But she's smiling and giggling and being all pathetic. "Okay. Okay. I love you. Say it back." She listens and then smiles again, lighting up her whole body. When she hangs up, she gives a deep giant sigh like you see girls do in the movies when they kind of take a couple seconds off from reality.

Then, like a light switch, she gets straight-faced and says, "'Fess up."

I don't want to. Or maybe I do. "You have to promise not tell Mom or especially not Dad."

"Of course. You know I would never tell the Units anything." Actually, I don't know that. I don't know that at all. . .but I tell her everything anyway.

"That little punk," Marna says. She's instantly incensed. "If I ever see him—You know what, I know his sister. She's like, in band. Plays French horn or some crap like that. Ooooh!" She's seething angry, I swear. "You should totally kick his butt."

"He's pretty tall," I say.

"So? Just kick him in the balls. You know karate."

"Okay," I say, as if, sure, I'll just go kick Robert Bullock in the testicles.

She puts a finger on my raw ear and in a soft, almost hurt voice, she says, "That looks like somebody's heart, a real-live heart, shattered all over your ear."

"It's not that bad. Really."

"Well. . .ooh! I hate that Robert Bullock!" And she's gone. She's calling Bucky back before the door even closes. I hear her telling her boyfriend everything: the human heart, French horn, kicking someone in the balls, all of it.

Girls have no problem just hauling off and tagging guys in their privates. For a girl, it's easy: Flick? Kick. It's over. The boy is on his knees, begging God for some clean air and to be able to pee again standing upright. I know girls have to wear bras and tampons and have babies, but sometimes, I swear, they really do have it easier.

CHAPTER FIFTEEN

The next day, I'm actually in a great mood because tonight is the first night of basketball tryouts. And, for whatever reason, Robert Bullock is not on the bus home. I'm nervous, yeah, but the idea of maybe making the team is just too awesome and I can't stop thinking about it. Being the shortest person to make the basketball team will take me from being the shortest kid in 8th grade to the most amazing short kid to ever hit the hardwood at Beck Jr. High. I'd be epic.

As soon as I get home from school, I'll grab my ball and shoot for over an hour. My plan is to wear my Dr. J jersey and headband; these will bring me luck on the court. Most people don't know that Julius Erving was only 6'3" in high school. Short by NBA standards, right? I mean, he ended up being 6'6" with hands bigger than most people's steering wheels, BUT, at some point in his life, he still probably felt a little short. Or shorter than he wanted to be. Like me.

I go to run upstairs and my mom, sitting at the dining room table with Marna, says, "Wait a minute, Buster. Get back down here."

Uh-oh. When she says, "Wait a minute, Buster," you know it's not good. It's the "Buster" part that lets me know I'm busted for something. As I slowly come back down the stairs, I'm trying to think of all my lies I've currently got circulating and which one she has discovered so that I can use the time walking from the stairway to the dining room to think about how to lie about the lie when she calls me on the lie. But there's no getting out of this one. She's got empty ripped-up cookie boxes in both hands. Marna is just grinning from ear-to-ear. My mom is relatively calm, like she's a tough detective who finally cracked the case.

I don't know what Marna has said or not said. I'm looking to take her lead, but it would not be beyond her to blame it all on me.

"Did you eat these cookies?" My mom holds up the box.

I'm nervous and I say, "What cookies?"

She shakes the boxes and yells, in stereo, "These cookies!"

"The Thin Mints," I 'fess up immediately.

"Uh-huh." She looks at my sister and at me like she's waiting for a full confession. I don't know what to say: *First we opened the boxes, and then we ate the cookies? Ah, then Marna broke out in hives and almost died, but she's in love, so...*

"Why?" she wants to know.

I don't know. "I don't know," I say.

"You don't know? Are you some kind of psychopath that just does things, that STEALS, without even thinking about it?!"

I shake my head, no. I've been through these situations enough to know when my mom asks questions like "are you some kind of psychopath?" we're really not supposed to answer the question. If I say, "No I'm not some kind of psychopath," she will yell, "But you are doing things that psychopaths do," and I don't really have a comeback to that. If I say, "Well, maybe I'm some kind of psychopath," she will think I'm making fun and get angrier and scream even louder, though I don't think that's possible.

"And you," she says, turning to Marna whose eyes are half open, glazed over, and has a really weird grin on her face. Marna could be a good serial killer, I've just decided. She's maybe too allergic to steal cookies for a living, but she could kill people and never flinch. "A Girl Scout that steals her own cookies?!"

Marna chokes back a laugh. Oh boy.

"I suppose breaking one of the Ten Commandments is a big joke to you?"

"No," she says, still stifling cracking up.

"Then can you explain why a 16-year-old would open two boxes of cookies and proceed to eat cookies she didn't pay for?"

"I wanted to see if I was still allergic to peanut butter," she says.

"Are you crazy?"

"Well, I didn't die, so, you know, there's that."

Man, I wish I could think of half the things Marna says. It's like my mom is so angry, but at the same time really impressed with the words that come out of her daughter's mouth too. That's probably not true, but maybe what I wish were true.

"What gives you, or you, the right to steal?"

"I don't know," I say. My stock answer.

"I don't know," my mom mimics me. "Well, who knows then?"

"I don't know," I say, because I don't know who knows.

"Nobody gives anybody the right to do anything anyway," Marna says. In my head, I'm like, *What?*

"What?" my mom asks.

"Just forget it," Marna spits back all attitudinal. "I'll pay it back."

"How?"

"I don't know. I'll babysit." Marna does babysit sometimes and sometimes comes home with about 40 bucks.

"I'll use my bar mitzvah money," I say. Which was stupid to say.

Because my mom is yelling at us, rattling my whole insides, I'm not thinking straight – I need to remember, my parents currently have no jobs. "You will NOT use your bar mitzvah money to pay back money you STOLE! That money is in the bank and off limits! I've told you this! Both of you make me sick!"

My mom's voice is ringing in my ears now because her yelling is able to reach that kind of deafening pitch. Seriously. And I can see the spit in her mouth and between her teeth, and her eyes bulging out of their sockets. Trust me, you don't want to make her angry, not even for a cool box of Thin Mints.

"Go to your rooms and wait for your father to come home."

And it hits me, like "duh." It's been a long time since we had to wait for my dad to come home. In other words, we're really in trouble here.

"But I'm meeting Jen at the mall. She's waiting for me," Marna pleads.

"She can wait from now until hell freezes over. You're not goin' anywhere, sister. Now, how do you like them apples?!"

For once in my life, I actually have someplace I'm supposed to be too, so I chime in, "But I have basketball tryouts, Mom. You said you'd drive me."

"I wouldn't drive you down the driveway to get the mail. I don't drive criminals. How do you like that, Buster? Now get out of my sight!"

We go. Marna is pissed, but not too pissed because after all, my mom sent her to her room, her favorite place in the world. That's like sending a bear to the forest for pooping in the woods. She slams her door, mostly for effect, and gets on the phone. She's talking to Bucky about my mom and how lucky he is to have his own place, and that being allergic to peanut butter was still the best thing she ever did in her lousy life.

Chapter Sixteen

Wait for your father to come home. Is there any worse way to spend time? I think I would rather go to Cherry Hill Mall and count to infinity. Really.

Things I'm thinking about while I wait for my father to come home:

- Will he beat me?
- If he beats me, how will he do it?
- Aren't I too old to be spanked?
- Will he spank Marna too?
- If I stole a car, would I still get spanked (you know, after jail)?
- What is Sara Rothman doing?
- Does Sara Rothman get spanked?
- NO WAY!!
- I hate Robert Bullock. I hate the bus.
- I wish I could have tried out for the basketball team.
- And. . .I'm somewhat relieved that I can't try out for the basketball team. Damn! There's no way I would have made it. Too short. Period.
- If I would have tried out for the basketball team and made it, I would have asked Monica Johnson to dance with me in PE. She would want to.

- Should I ask Monica Johnson to square dance? How?
- I wish Monica Johnson were Sara Rothman in disguise.
- Wait, does that make sense?
- Cookies. Thin Mints.
- I'm hungry.
- When my dad gets home from work, will he kiss my mom hello before she tells him that HIS kids stole Girl Scout cookies?
- Will he eat dinner first and then come up and beat me?
- I hate when my mom yells. Sometimes I'd rather be spanked and be done.
- What time is it?
- I could read a book, but why?
- I'm bored. I'm hungry. I feel sick to my stomach.
- My favorite part in The Who's *Baba O'Riley* is, "Don't cry, don't raise your eyes. . . It's only teenage wasteland." It's an old song, but it's a really good one.
- My ear still hurts from Bullock. A lot.
- I feel sick to my stomach but hungry at the same time. How is that even possible?
- I can't believe I'm not trying out for the basketball team. I really wanted to. Really. Want to. Even though I was nervous. Damn.

I'm a combination of bored and stressed so I can't sit still; but at the same time, I don't want to do anything because I can't focus. It's dark outside. Tryouts are over by now. Consider me cut.

"I didn't make the team," I say out loud to Snowball, who is lying next to me on my bed, his chin perched on my chest. He's a dog, I get that, but he almost looks worried for me, serious. And he knows what it's like to wait for my dad to come home. Back when he peed all over our brand new house, my dad spanked him with a rolled-up news-paper from my route. I know he was just trying to teach Snowball not to mark his territory all over our new rugs, but when you hear your dog, your best friend, yelp over and over after each thwap!, well. . .it's the worst sound in the world.

I go to my dresser, grab the box of letters I wrote this summer, and spill them on my bed. There's a stamp that says PEACE 49 cents on each letter. If that's all it costs, maybe I can scrape that up from my piggy bank and give it to my dad when he comes for me. On the back of every envelope I had actually put the date, so while I wait for my father, I decide to arrange the letters in chronological order.

It feels like forever, but I hear my dad get home and my mom tell him what happened, though I can't make out exactly what she's saying. The only thing I can make out is something like, ". . .your son," and "breaking the Ten Commandments," and then I hear him sighing like he does when he's all stressed. Sometimes I try to imagine why my parents even had kids. Really. I mean, they try to do all these things and we just disappoint them. And it's not like my dad just got home from "work," because he currently doesn't have a job. According to my mom, his job is to look for another job or part-time jobs until he gets his real job back. Which can't be a fun job at all.

My dad opens my door without knocking because. . .he can. I'm so nervous that suddenly I'm no longer hungry.

I just want it to be tomorrow because then whatever he's going to do will be done, and if I'm still alive, at least I'll know what was done. People might think that it's the waiting that really sucks, but it's this, right now, him here.

"I've come to beat you," he says. And while he's not laughing, it's my dad so it's still kind of funny. But, again, he's not laughing.

"You don't have to," I say. I'm not sure if I tell him this because I don't want to get beaten because, well, it will hurt. . . or because I'm trying to let my dad know that I've got the message. I've learned my lesson: never listen to Marna.

"Let us begin," he says. I can't tell what's going on. He's like a robot all of the sudden. He was given his orders and the only way he won't carry them through is if somebody unplugs him.

"I'll never eat Girl Scout cookies again," I say out of desperation. "Even, even if I have the money."

"The crime was committed and the crime must be punished."

I stand up, and without even thinking it through, I start to unbuckle my belt. It's been at least a year I think since I've gotten an official spanking, but still, I know how this goes. I remember.

"I'll be needing that," my dad says. So I give him my belt. After I take my lucky shirt off, I unbutton my Levis 501s and take them off. I go to take my underwear off because I can't remember if I'm supposed to offer my naked butt or just to my underwear. My dad nods no. So, I'm naked except for my Fruit of the Looms. He twists my belt so he can hold it like a whip and lifts his head to see me there, almost all naked. This is what a spanking is. You wait all day in your room and think about it. I'm almost relieved that the waiting part is over.

I peek up at my dad's eyes for a second and then away. He doesn't have his robot look on anymore. He's thinking, running his unbelted hand through his bald head. Besides my embarrassment of being almost naked and wanting to put my clothes back on, I feel kind of bad for my dad: He has to hurt me.

I remember in Hebrew School learning about these Jews who were organized by the Nazis to be like a Jewish police service against other Jews in the ghettos during the Holocaust. My teacher said they were called Judenrat. These were Jews who were spared going to concentration camps and becoming slaves, but they had to do a lot of the dirty work for the Gestapo. Sometimes they had to be violent to fellow Jews, to people they grew up with in their own neighborhoods. In some sense, my dad is the mongrel sent up here to be violent to his only son. That's gotta suck after a long day at work trying to find work. He probably just wants to eat dinner.

The whole thing takes me over and I begin to cry without making a sound. I mean, I know I said I don't cry, and I swear I'm trying not to because I also know if I cry it makes it worse for him. So I suck it back up. That's where they get that phrase I'm sure, "suck it up." I'm sucking it up. Besides, I want to show him I'm a *man* and I can take it.

He tells me to lie across my bed with my butt in the air. I stare at my rubber King Kong doll on my night table that I got from Disney World when I was 6 years old, and I clench my teeth together as hard as possible. And wait for it.

Nothing.

I clench my teeth and close my eyes. And wait.

Nothing.

"Put your pants back on," he says as he looks out my window and places the belt on my night table, next to Kong.

"What?"

"Your pants."

"Why?"

"Just. . .Just do it."

And it finally occurs to me that I'm not going to get beaten. I'm relieved for a couple seconds. Then I start to feel bad again for my dad. He just seems different, like defeated – permanently defeated. Maybe because he doesn't really have a job right now, I don't know. Like, he was sent up here to do a job by the commander in chief, and he didn't get it done. If he was a Jewish soldier in the Gestapo, a Judenrat, ordered to beat me and didn't, then *he'd* get the beating. Or worse.

"You want me to scream or something? Like you're hurting me?" And I start crying again even though I'm trying really hard to suck it up.

"We need to discuss the proper punishment for stealing," my dad says really soft.

"Okay," I say, trying like hell to stop whimpering.

"It's lying," he says, still looking out the window and talking like he just lost the big game. "And then you lied about stealing, which is. . ." He can't even finish, that's how disgusted he is at me.

"Yeah, I know that." That's my dad's number one rule. Don't lie. No matter what. If he were running for president of the United States, his slogan would be, *vote for Dan Ratner – don't lie to me and I won't lie to you.*

"I'll pay the Girl Scouts back."

"You bet you will."

"And, and I didn't get to try out for the basketball team either," I say, to offer up a natural consequence, but saying it makes me start crying again.

My dad looks at me, up and down like Mr. Cunningham, and nods. I don't think he thought I was going to make the team anyway, which is not why I'm crying. Damn. Or maybe it is. Damn. I can tell he thinks I caught him looking me up and down and he's back at my window, staring at our back yard. I want him to say, "After you're finished being grounded. . .you get back out there. Practice. Take, I don't know, 500 shots a day. . . Try out next year. Make that deal with yourself. No matter what."

But he doesn't. He just keeps looking out the window and says, "This one. . .this one breaks my heart, son."

He turns around because he's done, and goes to Marna's room.

I should be relieved because my father didn't beat me, but instead I'm incredibly sad. Even Snowball can tell. He jumps on my lap and rubs his cheesy ear against my chest, as we both watch my dad leave my room sort of empty handed. "Everything's gonna be different now," I tell Snowball, and let my face flop into his puffy head. I don't know exactly how it'll be different. . .just that it will be.

CHAPTER SEVENTEEN

I t's short and sweet. Marna is on the phone when my dad walks in her room without knocking. He says nothing.

"Excuse me, I'm on the phone," she says. I mean that's Marna. When she has to wait for my father to come home, she doesn't even think about it. My father walks right up to her and grabs her phone from her ear, hangs up on whoever it is on the other end (Bucky!) and she's like, "Hey!" And then he stuffs the phone into his front pocket and leaves. He went right for her jugular – no, her heart. As he walks down the stairs with her heart in his front pocket, Marna opens her door and screams, as loud as my mom at least, "I hate. . ." and then she stops to adjust her volume because she hears my dad stop in the middle of the stairs, ". . . living here!" She goes back into her room and slams the door. The whole house shakes.

"Dan?" My mom anxiously calls after my dad, who I believe throws Marna's phone in the kitchen garbage can.

"Just a second, Dear," he says as he goes into the garage. From my bedroom, I hear him shuffling around in there. Before I know it, my dad is back upstairs with his electric screwdriver. I swear it takes him like four seconds to unscrew all of the screws that attach Marna's door to its frame. He literally takes Marna's door *off* of her room. This I've never seen before. Marna is speechless, until she finally says, "Hey, what are you doin'? You can't do that."

I watch the whole thing, shocked. With the door in his hands, he heaves it over his head so that it switches from vertical to horizontal and he makes his way downstairs, the door in his clutches. I thought a big door would be really heavy, but my dad tosses it over his shoulders easily, lighter than a bag of laundry. Maybe he has adrenalin left over in his body from not beating us.

"In my house," my dad says before heading down the rest of the stairs, "we don't slam things."

My sister and I are in the hallway with our big cookie-eating mouths wide open, staring at each other. Then she huffs, turns and goes back to her bed. I stay in the hallway because I want to listen to my mom when my dad walks by with a big door in his hands.

"Dan, would you stop a second and tell me what happened?" she pleads.

He stops, sets the door down: Thud. "I beat the children, Dear."

I didn't come down for dinner. I basically fell asleep with my clothes on and my belt and King Kong doll in my hands.

TATTOO SHOW-N-TELL #2
INSTALLMENT

*A*nd this here on my other arm is a tattoo of my ex-wife, Angie. It's there to remind me of all the mistakes I've made in my life. And because I'm too chicken to get it removed.

Okay then, sit back, sit down, and sit up straight. Here we go.

CHAPTER EIGHTEEN

B ecause I'm still grounded, I only go to school, karate, and
now Sunday school. I'm nervous to go to Mrs. Rubin's
Jewish Cultures class because Monica Johnson will be there.
So will Robert Bullock. I can't believe I share the same religion with that guy. Mrs. Rubin's post bar mitzvah class has
a pretty big reputation for talking about meaty issues like
what Jews think about marriage and sex. At least that's how
Marna described it.

I take a seat two seats behind Monica, but then Robert
sits right behind me.

On the first day, Mrs. Rubin decides to show us this documentary of some of the concentration camps where they
took the Jews, gypsies, and other doomed people during
WWII. Which is not about sex or marriage at all.

Robert flicks my ear when Mrs. Rubin switches off the
lights to start the film. "Hey, Ratner, short people were con-
sidered gypsies. Betcha didn't know that. Sorry."

Before Mrs. Rubin starts the film, she hesitates and says,
"Guys," (she calls all of us "Guys" like we're her friends),
"This stuff is pretty rough. . .but you're as ready as you can
be. . ." I'm like, just show us the movie. I mean I've been
watching R-rated stuff, classic horror flicks—*Amityville
Horror, The Shining,* and *Alien* (hello? The alien literally pops
out of the dude's stomach!)—and those flicks are scary, but

not so much to where I'm having nightmares or running out of the room crying. It's all pretend crap anyway.

But this movie isn't make-believe. It's a documentary, and Mrs. Rubin says, "Some of the footage was taken by the Germans to show the rest of the world how things were just peachy in the work camps. The Russians, though, also shot footage after the war ended and concentration camp survivors were liberated. So some of this is pretty intense. Okay?"

Mrs. Rubin starts the film, and like a car crash, I can't believe what I'm watching. As a person who loves horror movies and karate-ninja movies, and especially movies where things blow up a lot, this Holocaust movie is the scariest flick I've ever seen. And not just because I'm Jewish.

Mrs. Rubin stops and starts the film, explaining all these different scenes. Now, people are lined up, being shot one by one just because they are too old or weak to work. There's no sound like in regular movies where you hear the gun shot. Seeing it in black and white and NOT hearing makes it so real that it's not real. But it doesn't *feel* like a real movie either; I guess because it all really happened.

Another scene shows the Gestapo quickly divide all of these people into two different groups. Some members of a family go into one group and onto one train, and other members board a different train. Everyone is also automatically divided into males and females too, so Mrs. Rubin says, "When they say goodbye to their moms and their sisters, that was it. They likely would never see them again."

The next scene shows a baby being taken from its mother, both of them crying. Screaming. There's no sound again, but it feels like the sound is echoing, even louder because you can't hear it, if that makes any sense.

The train cars are so crowded tight that there's no place for anyone to sit, but people continue to be herded on the train. And Mrs. Rubin says, "Their strategy was to make the Jews feel like they were no longer human." She explains how they would travel for days on the train that was locked from the outside and get no food at all.

Click, the movie continues. Another scene:

SS soldiers dump all these suitcases at the train station, while others rummage through the piles of stuff, looking for valuables. And at the camps they have these doctors who pull teeth that have gold or silver fillings in them. Can you imagine having a tooth pulled with no Novocain at all? Other doctors do evil experiments on people, like slice off their skin to make soap, or remove their whole fingernails; crap like that just to see what would happen. Mrs. Rubin says the main doctor was Dr. Mengele. That name even sounds like a crazy doctor.

But the part that gets Monica Johnson is the giant graves the SS dig. Apparently, the SS would shoot hundreds of Jews at one time, and then throw them into a gigantic pile, like stacks of sticks, and light the pile on fire by pouring gasoline all over them. Sometimes they would use a bulldozer to shove the people into one big hole in the ground. A giant grave. The thing that gets me, and I guess gets Monica too, is that some of the shot-up people aren't all the way dead yet. Some are still breathing, but bulldozers drop tons of dirt on their heads.

"Sometimes," says Mrs. Rubin, "a wounded person would take a better pair of shoes off of a dead person as they climbed their way out of the pile of dead to possible freedom. Others were just stuck, or too wounded to move, and be buried alive."

Well, when Mrs. Rubin mentions being buried alive, a bawling Monica, bolts out of class.

I want to admit this right now that when Monica dashed for the bathroom to throw up or clean up or just apply more make-up, I couldn't help thinking about how good she looks in her jeans. Even though Monica wears these tight designer jeans that look like she paints them on (that's how Marna describes it), she still walks very fast, especially when she's bawling and bolting out of class, so she never looks like she's cramped or uncomfortable. Which is good.

Mrs. Rubin doesn't chase after Monica or yell at her for leaving the room without a pass. She clicks the movie back on and soon after, Monica comes back and takes her seat. Her eyes are all swollen and she's got a tissue. Mrs. Rubin doesn't say anything to her, but as she's walking around the room like teachers do, she pats Monica's back. Monica looks up, sniffling, and smiles at Mrs. Rubin.

I imagine crying Monica Johnson square dancing with me; her chipmunk cheeks and watery eyes, plus her amazing, tight jeans. . . and I would tap her on her back and she would sniff and smile at me too.

Then Robert Bullock actually raises his hand and asks, "If they are locked in these animal cars for a week, then where do they take a leak or even, you know, go number two?" This makes everyone sort of laugh, but not all the way like you might think.

But Mrs. Rubin is so cool, the kind of teacher that can't be thrown off her game. She says, "Good question. Let me ask you a question, Robert. Where do cows go to the bathroom if they're on a cargo train and they have to go?"

"A cow would just. . ." Robert stops talking. He looks around the room like he wants help or sympathy from his own people for what he just discovered about, well, his own people. And here I am, an idiot. . .I should revel in the idea of Robert suffering in front of the whole room, even if it's just for a second. . .but, suddenly, and I don't know why, I feel sorry for him. It's the closest thing to flicking Robert Bullock back on his ear that I'm gonna get, and instead, I feel bad. What's wrong with me?

CHAPTER NINETEEN

The good news? I found out Robert Bullock didn't make the 8th grade basketball team. The bad news? Robert Bullock didn't make the 8th grade basketball team. So instead of attending practice after school, he rides the bus home with me.

It's gone from just messing around to slow torture. To put it another way, I have daydreamed about hitting Robert Bullock with a baseball bat to break his skull wide open. Wouldn't that be great? Break his skull open and put new brains in his head. Brains that tell him to sit someplace else.

I hate the bus. I wish I lived right behind the school like Kevin. I could just walk by myself, or even with Kevin, and this whole thing would be nothing.

Speaking of Kevin, I haven't seen him since basketball tryouts ended. He made the team, of course, but I usually see him between fourth and fifth periods in the hallway getting something out of his locker and then typically before I get on the bus. I guess after school, he has to go to basketball practice. I don't know. I've called him a couple times on the weekends to maybe go shoot around, but nobody is ever home. He never calls me back. It's probably nothing, but who knows what he hears about me now?

"Look who didn't even try out for the team; it's Raaaaatner," Robert Bullock says. "Whatchou gotta say now, Rrrrrratner?"

"Nothing." I'm dead in the middle of the bus. Devon and all of Robert Bullock's friends are in the back. Why does he sit down right next to me then? I just want to go home. I hate school. I hate the bus. I hate Robert Bullock. I just want to watch *Sponge Bob* and space out. Get out of my head. Seriously.

He flicks my ear, lightly (if that's possible), and laughs. "That's what I thought, Ratner." I just try to ignore him and look out the window. I watch the street go by as we roll. Two more stops until Robert gets off the bus.

"Hey Ratner. Hey Ratner." He won't let me ignore him. And when I don't turn around, he flicks me harder. Just a flick. Not a punch. I turn and look at him. I think about staying in control—"Oooh, Ratner," he says. "You're not mad, are you? Watch out. Ratner's mad. Ratner's angry." He cracks up.

I look up at the rearview mirror and see the bus driver's eyes on us. He's staring a bit while kids get off at a stop. One more stop and Robert Bullock leaves. The bus driver, as usual, says nothing. I want to repeat the word "Bullock" to him over and over until he gets sick of his own name too.

The bus stops and Robert gets up to leave. "C'mon Ratner, we're just having fun here. Let's shake on it. It's a long year. We gotta be able to tell jokes. C'mon, Ratner."

I go to shake his hand and he pulls it away and cracks up. Another joke.

He's laughing and people are watching. . . of course. They are always watching even when they're not watching. "Alright, c'mon, shake on it."

I don't.

"Now you're creating bad feelings here, Ratner. Thought we were friends. Buddies." He laughs and flicks my ear. I know it's coming so I jerk my head to avoid it, but he connects with my neck instead. Hurts. Stings. And it's gonna leave a mark.

"Ooooh, you're fast, Ratner. Tricky. Sneaky Rat—ner!" He says on his way down the bus stairs. "Raaaaaaaaaaaatner!"

He's gone.

The rest of the bus ride I just cave into my seat, my hand covering the flicked part of my neck, and breathe. Feels like I'd been holding my breath the whole ride.

I want to call Monica Johnson when I get home. I have her number from our Hebrew School class roster. I have Robert Bullock's number too for that matter. I wish I could call and ask his parents to teach their son to sit next to somebody his own size.

On the same phone list is Sara Rothman's old phone number, and sadly, her new international phone number. I wish her old number was her only number and I'd be calling that number when I got home.

But if I can call Monica and set up something before we start the square dance unit, then maybe I could fight Robert Bullock, you know? Or maybe he would find out that I'm dancing with Monica Johnson and he would back off because then I'd be somewhat cool. Screw it, if Monica Johnson agrees to be my partner, then I would *have* to beat up Robert Bullock. I'd just do it, even if I had to kick him in the nuts. I'd even promise Snowball. No way is he going to screw-up me and Monica Johnson. No way.

I have to call her as soon as I get home. I have to.

CHAPTER TWENTY

M arna is on the phone, of course. I'm not sure if her and Bucky ever got off the phone last night. Really. See, last night Marna came home and placed a wad of cash on the dining room table and informed my parents that she paid the price for the stolen cookies, and also demanded her cell phone back. She said if she were going to be grounded, restricted from society, she would need to stay connected to society. Otherwise, according to her, it would officially be parental abuse. My parents were sort of shocked by this declaration, or maybe by my sister quoting directly from an article about these kids who were locked in a basement for two years until police found out and arrested the parents on abuse charges.

"Well, that doesn't apply here," my dad said. "You don't even have a door."

"I'll be needing that back too. The same research suggests that teenagers experience the most physical growth during this time period. To sleep and get dressed without a door is not only creepy, it's a form of abuse. I'll need it back."

Sometimes my parents just don't have the kind of energy to fight back. I understand that completely.

Later that night, while Marna was talking on her phone, my dad reattached her door. When I fell asleep last night,

Marna was on the phone with Bucky. And before I left for the bus stop, she was on the phone with Bucky, and she's on the phone right now. I think it could be my turn. Believe it or not, my sister and I share "her" cell phone, but since I never want to talk on it and she always does, it's never been a problem. Until now.

"Marna, I have to use the phone," I say.

"Hold on," she says to Bucky. "What?"

"I have to make an important call. I just need the phone for a couple of minutes." If my parents were home from work, I could ask to use one of their cell phones, but then they'll ask who I want to call, and I really don't want to answer that question. I need to call Monica before this house gets busy with nosy people.

"Okay. Jeez." To the phone she says, "He's a little hyper today." To me, "I'll be off soon."

"Good. Good. 'Cause I need the phone."

My ear is sort of ringing a bit from Robert's power flicks, so I go take a look in the mirror. The lobe is definitely aflame, but what I can't believe is my neck. Looks like a giant suck-smooch. It's red, sure, but it's already got some black and blue around the edges of the red part. I'm so pissed. I'm not a big fan of hickeys. I mean it seems stupid to literally suck somebody's neck like a vampire. But at least if I'm going to have a hickey, it should be because a girl, like Monica Johnson or Sara Rothman or even Jillian Lipshultz, gives it to me. Not because Robert Bullock flicks it on me.

Marna is still on the phone. I can't take it and I burst into her room:

"I NEED TO USE THE PHONE!!! PLEASE! I SAID PLEASE! I NEVER WANT TO USE THE PHONE BUT NOW I DO SO COULD YOU PLEASE GET OFF THE FLIPPIN' PHONE!"

While I'm ranting and raving, Marna says hold on to Bucky and turns the phone away from her ear so that he can hear me freak out. She sneaks in something like, "My brother has gone wack-a-do. Can you hear him?"

My maniacal yell for the phone clearly doesn't faze my sister one bit, although she is kind of staring at me all of a sudden like I'm from outer space.

"Oh my God!" Marna practically screams as she leans into me, right up to my neck. "You've got a hickey!"

"No I don't," I say, smacking my hand over the flick mark on my throat.

"Buck, Buck, my little brother here has a hickey," she says to the phone. "Of course he needs the phone. He needs to call his new honey." I hear Bucky launch some sort of cowboy yelp through the phone. Marna points at my neck and says, "That's an authentic suck mark. Impressive, little brother."

"No I don't. I mean—I don't have a hickey!"

My sister leans in even closer and looks again.

"Buck, let me call you right back." And she hangs up. Just like that.

"It's not!" I blurt out, covering my neck. "Stop! It's nowhere near a hickey!"

"Okay, okay, calm down. Man, you're hyper today. Let me see."

I let her see because I don't want to tell her. She gets up to it with one eye and finally says, "You're right. It's not. There's no central suck mark. No nucleus. Unless you were smooching with a girl that has an upper lip and no lower lip."

"I toldja. Now, can I use the phone?" Thing is, I don't even want to call Monica Johnson anymore. I did, but I don't now. I just feel lousy.

When I look up, I see that Marna has small tears welling up and then a few trickle down her cheeks. She sniffles and finally asks, "He. . . did this to you?"

I look away.

"God!" She pounds her fist against the wall. "I'll kill that little punk!"

"You better not tell Mom and Dad," I jump in. "Promise you won't tell Mom and Dad, Marna. You have to promise."

"Why? Why can't I tell our parents?"

"You know why. She'll want to call the principal and the bus driver and the president of the United States, and Dad will start spewing stories about all the tall kids he beat up when he was my age. I just don't need that right now. Okay?"

"Can I tell Bucky?"

"You already did."

"Oh."

And my sister, tears gently rolling down her face, slowly, tenderly, hands over the phone. She hasn't given me the phone in five years I don't think. And then she gives me something else: a hug, and I clearly don't know what I'm supposed to do with it. I'm just a dude with a fake hickey, holding a phone.

CHAPTER TWENTY-ONE

At dinner, everyone is quiet. I'm wearing a turtleneck. It still has tags. It's purple.

Marna finally breaks the silence, "So it's definitely gonna happen?"

The "it" she's talking about is the Philadelphia School District teachers striking for the entire school year. In other words, cancelling the whole school year.

"Looks that way," my dad says, exhaling this huge sigh of stress.

"Why don't the teachers ever strike in our district?" I ask. I wish I could go to school in Philadelphia so that I wouldn't have to go to school.

"Because you live in a good neighborhood now. With good schools and good teachers and Jewish people," my mom says, like she's convincing the whole world and herself. "Because we make sacrifices so you don't have to miss school."

"Well don't do me any favors, Mom," Marna laughs. And I laugh. My parents don't. They don't laugh or smile or anything much lately. I see my mom give my dad a look, which makes him set his fork down, lean back in his chair and put his hands behind his head how he does when he's about to say something to the group.

He clears his throat and begins like it's a lecture, "It has come to our attention, son, that you may be having some difficulties at school."

"I can't believe you told them," I say to Marna, dropping my fork hard.

"I didn't. I just said you don't have a hickey. Remember when I got in so much trouble when I had a hickey—ah, allegedly—can I be excused now? Please?"

"No," both my mom and dad say in unison.

"We live here, Larry," my mom says. "We see how you are." She dabs her lips with her napkin and softly says, "And we miss your smile."

"You're not a happy kid anymore and that concerns us," my dad says.

"You need to know, Larry, that these morons who choose to pick on you because maybe you're a smaller kid have a low self-esteem," my mom says.

"Yeah, that should really comfort him," Marna says.

"What's that supposed to mean?" my mom shoots back at Marna.

"It's just that you always say that if someone picks on you it's because they don't like themselves."

"It's true," my mom says.

"Yup," chimes in Dad. "A person who likes himself doesn't need to put somebody else down to make himself feel better."

"That may be true," says Marna, "but they still do it. What's he supposed to say after they flick 'im in the ear? 'Ah ha! Caught ya! You don't like yourself, nanny-nanny-poo-poo'?"

This makes us all laugh, even my mom for a moment, but then she looks at my dad as if to say, get on with the lecture.

"I think I should maybe call the principal about this boy who's harassing you," she finally announces.

"No!" I realize that my response is probably way too loud. "No, Mom. . .Please. That will make it worse." I give Marna a death stare. "So just don't, okay? Now can we move on to another dinner topic?"

"Well, okay. But your mother and I would like to help you." I can tell my dad is uncomfortable saying this because it means his son isn't tough like he was.

"Calling the principal is *not* going to help," I say. "That's the opposite of help."

"Maybe I should contact the boy's parents—"

"No, mom," I plead. "Please don't do that. Promise you won't do that."

"Or the bus driver," my dad says, trying to contribute.

Marna laughs.

"What's so funny?" My mom wants to know.

"Nothing. Just everybody knows bus drivers can't do crap. They have to pay attention to the road let alone deal with what's going on in the back of the bus."

"Maybe don't sit in the back of the bus, Larry," my mom says.

"Look, okay? It doesn't matter where I sit. And. . .and I should be able to sit wherever I want to sit anyways."

"He's right about that," my dad says with a little umph to it, almost macho even.

"Well I want to know how we're going to handle this problem." My mom is aggravated, which happens so easily. Especially lately.

"When I was your age, I was the smallest kid on my block just like you—"

"I know, Dad." I say, getting frustrated. Here it comes.

"Dan," my mom interrupts. "Stop."

"What? I'm just trying to help—"

"We get suspended for fighting," I blurt out. "You want me to get suspended?"

My mom says, "no" and my dad says, "yes," at the same time.

"No," my mom says, staring down my dad for a second.

"Of course not," he says, surrendering. Silence. And then: "But, sometimes. . ."

"But what?" My mom wants him to continue. Which is sort of odd.

"He who can't learn must feel," he says. "That's all I was trying to say before."

"No," my mom says, all weird. Clearly struggling. "Now let's be clear. You had a temper. There's a difference."

"Okay, fine," my dad says. Not angry or anything, but deliberate. "But I was short, like Larry. And when a bigger kid picked on me, I hit him." My dad glares at me. "First. Always. And kept hitting him until somebody pulled me off of him. Which someone always does."

"So, what?" I say. "You're saying that it's okay if I get in trouble for fighting?"

My mom looks at my dad, and then shuffles her fork around her mashed potatoes kind of like Marna does with her food. She looks down at her food and says, "We're saying that we'd be okay to pick you up from school if we get a call that you've been in a fight. There. End of discussion." She puts a forkful of mashed potatoes in her mouth.

"Cool," Marna exclaims.

"Not you," my mom says with her mouth full.

I take a giant gulp of milk, relieved that the discussion about me is over.

"God, Larry gets everything," Marna says, half-kidding.

"You can have this," my mom says and then sticks her tongue out with the chewed up mashed potatoes on it. Gross.

My dad chews up some meat and opens his mouth to show his food to the whole table, and with his mouth wide open says to Marna, "No fighting."

Milk starts to seep through my teeth, but I can't hold it anymore, so it spews out of my mouth and the rest escapes through my nostrils and splashes onto the Ratner dinner table. Classic.

It feels good to really laugh hard. I don't think I have since my bar mitzvah.

Tattoo Show-N-Tell #3. . .
November Installment

*A*nd this here on my other arm is a tattoo of my other ex-wife, also named Angie. But she made me spell in all capital letters. It's there to remind me of all the mistakes I've made in my life. And because I'm too chicken to get it erased. Well, it hurts to get 'em erased.

Okay then, sit back, sit down, and sit up straight. Here we go.

CHAPTER TWENTY-TWO

I still haven't called Monica and the square dancing unit starts tomorrow.

"Square dancing," Mr. Stack says and smiles. We all moan. Even if you don't mind dancing in front of people, which I do, and even if you're not scared to ask girls to dance, which I am, nobody would rather square dance than play football or war ball or even soccer. PE is and never has been a place for dancing.

"Men! The time has come! OH YES! IT'S A SQUARE, MEN!"

All of a sudden, I see Kevin give Mr. Stack a pass. While Mr. Stack reads the pass, moving his lips while he's reading, Kevin looks out at the class and gives a couple of nods to some of the guys on the basketball team. He sees me, I think, but doesn't nod. I hate when you think someone sees you and they don't even act like they see you.

Mr. Stack signs the pass and tells Kevin to go sit down. What? Is he in my PE class now? He doesn't sit by me. Instead he goes by where all the basketball players are sitting; a bunch of tall kids with big shoes in the back.

Mr. Stack's neck veins are back full of blood, just like we learned in science, how veins get all bloated and pop out. We dissect frogs, not PE teachers, but somehow bloody veins came up and I remembered because of Mr. Stack.

"Now tomorrow, boys – tomorrow is a big day. Huge!"
More moans.

He talks really soft and low. "You can ask a girl from Ms. Gimp's class to be your partner, and if she's stupid enough—I mean kind enough—to agree, then you're set. But you must have a partner. If you can't find your own partner, then you'll be partnerin' up with me. Do I make myself clear?"

"WHO WANTS TO DANCE WITH MR. STACK?!!"

"Not me!" we all say. Some people say, "No one does." I hear Kevin make his voice into a girly voice and say, "I do." This cracks up the whole class. He gets a bunch of high fives from all of the basketball players.

It takes me three times of dialing on my lock before my locker finally opens. I dress in. That's what you do after PE. You dress *out* for class and then dress back *in* afterward. No one ever takes a shower even though we're supposed to. I try to wear shirts that are really long to school which isn't hard to do for me. Typically, I put my shirt on first so it covers my stuff, and then I get my pants on as soon as humanly possible without looking like I'm trying not to be naked in a hurry. But today, before I can get my pants on, I hear a *thwap!* and feel a sting on the back of my leg. It's Kevin, laughing, twirling his towel up, getting it ready to launch again.

"Gotcha!" Kevin says, smiling. "So I guess I'm in your PE class."

"How come?" I ask, back in my locker, trying not to over-react to anything.

"Coach Cunningham wants all the basketball players in this PE hour."

"Oh."

"I thought you were going to try out for the team too."

"I was." I pull up my pants, my face still in my locker. "I couldn't get a ride."

"That's why you gotta live in cheap-o apartments behind school like me."

"Yeah. Well." I button my pants and close my locker.

"Alright, Ratner. Big day tomorrow. Monica Johnson. She's hot. Ask her. Don't mess that up. Did I mention she's hot?"

"Yeah. Who are you gonna ask?"

"You don't never know, Ratner," he says smiling. "I wish your sister went to this school." He winks and snaps the towel at me one more time, making me hop back into my locker to barely avoid the whack, but the percussion of me hitting the metal echoes throughout the locker room, and then Kevin's around the corner laughing and giving high fives to his teammates. Did they send him over to snap me with a towel? And why is he calling me *Ratner* now? And what does he mean, *don't mess that up?* I would think that Kevin coming into PE would be a good thing, to have a friend in a class, but everything is so weird lately. And now he can see things that I'm not sure I want him to see.

Kevin is amazing though. He just shows up in the middle of the school year in the middle of a new class and fits right in. I can't even take the bus home.

CHAPTER TWENTY-THREE

As soon as I get home from karate I'm going to call
Monica and ask her to be my partner for tomorrow.
I have to. And if she says yes, then, I swear, I will destroy
Robert Bullock on the bus tomorrow. I'll just keep hitting
him until somebody pulls me off.

It's confusing, though, because here I am in karate
learning how to fight. Like, today we had to spar and I actually won against this 9th grader, who of course, was two feet
taller than me. He kept trying to front kick me in the gut to
score points, but his kicks were slow, I guess, and I blocked
them. And then one time, instead of blocking his kick, I
stepped to the left, spun and landed a back kick while his
leg was still up in the air trying to front kick me – but I
wasn't there! I yelped like you're supposed to, and threw a
punch to the face (not connecting of course!) for the win.
And, it was fun because it was like a game, a contest, not
flicking someone's ear. Or neck. Or some angry thing.

"Mr. Ratner?" Sensei calls to me as I pass his office on
the way out the door. That's how he addresses all of us – Mr.
This, Ms. That. Always all respectful. He's also pretty awesome at karate. When he yelps, or kiaps, it shakes all the butterflies in your stomach so much so that they pee in their
little butterfly pants. Serious.

"Come," he says. He smiles as he points to the chair on the other side of his desk. "Have a seat, Mr. Ratner."

I do. I've never had a one-on-one conversation with this quiet beast. He leans back in his seat with his hands behind his head, kind of like my dad does after a good meal, only my dad will unbutton the top button of his pants first.

"So? How are you doing?" Even this simple greeting is intimidating as hell.

"Good," I say.

"Good," he smiles. "How's school?"

"Good." I hope he can see I'm confused as to why he's calling me into his office. What did I do? Did my parents forget to pay the bill? Did I lose my scholarship? What?

"Good. Good, Mr. Ratner. Yes, do good in school. Important to do good."

We both say "good" a lot for no good reason.

"I hear you're having some trouble in school with a bully?" Or maybe I don't want to know the point. The word "bully" echoes in my brain.

"Oh, no," I say, fidgeting. Suddenly this chair is way uncomfortable. "Well, I mean, it's no, ah, trouble. Just, my mom worries a lot about, ah, nothing."

"Moms have a right to worry about their kids, no?"

"No. Yes. I mean yes. Yes. Right?"

"We teach about respect and integrity and honesty and commitment, no?"

I'm catching on that "No?" means "Right?" or even "Yes," but I just nod.

"People who make fun of other people are really making fun of themselves, no?"

"Yes."

"Why?"

"I don't know."

"No?"

"I mean, my mom says that they don't feel good about themselves if they have to make fun of other people."

"Ah. Your mom is a smart cookie, no?"

"Yes."

The sensei brings his arms out from behind his head and crosses them on the desk as he leans forward to talk to me.

"Mr. Ratner, it doesn't matter how big a person is physically." This time he asks me directly, "Right?"

"Right."

"How big are you in here?" He thumps his chest, his heart. It's not a question for me to answer. "And here." He points to his temples, smiles, and says, "You control your thoughts. You can be as big as a bear. . .and a bully can be as small as the smallest ant."

"Thank you, sir." I almost stand up to leave, but then I don't.

"Mr. Ratner?" He leans across his desk and curls both his hands into fists. If this chair had a back door, I would give a loud kiap and disappear. "We don't act out in anger," he says. His eyes are ultra magnets, forcing mine to stare back at his. "Control. Control your anger. Anger is for the weak."

"Yes, sir." I start to feel squirrelly, and I can't find a right way to sit.

"I have taught you. I have seen you learn."

"Thank you—"

"Do not interrupt, please," he says. Oh boy, is he angry at me? Then he smiles. Sometimes when I get nervous, I talk or laugh or feel like the butterflies in my stomach are all hyper, like they've been eating too much candy.

"I want to tell you that you know what to do, no?" I almost say "no" right back because I really *don't* know what to do. I'm confused by all of it. He stands up, motioning for me to stand up too. He bows to me, looking me in my eyes. And I bow back to him. The only thing I *do* know is that I really don't know what to do.

CHAPTER TWENTY-FOUR

I don't have to bribe Marna for the phone with Girl Scout cookies because she's at Girl Scouts when I come home from karate. Well, my parents *think* she's at Girl Scouts. She's actually probably with Bucky.

And I don't play that game where you dial and hang up and dial and hang up and dial and hang up. Instead, I just hyperventilate before calling Monica's number. I wait until 7:45, when hopefully she's eaten dinner and it's not too late. There's a ring. If I hang up now I'll probably go to hell; that is, if we believed in it.

"Hello?" I say, maybe loud enough to be heard. "Is Monica there?"

"May I ask who is calling please?" Wait. It sounds like Monica.

"It's Larry Ratner. . .ah, from Hebrew school." Why did I say from Hebrew school? Girls don't want to square dance with guys from Hebrew school.

There's a pause. "Larry?" she asks, totally not believing I'm on her phone. "For real? Larry?" I nod yes. Pretty stupid. "How'd you get my number?"

Uh-oh. "Ah, I got it from the list."

"What list?"

I don't want to say Hebrew school again. "You know. The list they give all the parents."

I hear a girl laughing in the background.

"What are you doin'?" I ask.

"Oh," she laughs and I can tell it's really Monica. "Me and my sister are trying to figure out all the songs with the word *eye* in them," she says. "Not the pronoun I, eye like eyeball eye." I hear more cackling in the background, namely her younger sister, Sylvia, who also goes to my Hebrew school. "Wait, what? Oh. Sylvia wants to know what color Kelly Clarkson's *eyes* really are behind those hazel eyes? Do you know?"

"Oh. Ah. I'm not sure." God, what a lame answer to a question.

"Sylvia wants to know what good are you then?"

"What?" I ask, and hear more laughing. I hate people in the background. I wonder if anybody ever has a private conversation on this planet.

"She's just kidding," Monica says, giggling while also trying to shush her sister.

"Oh. That's, that's—that hurt," I say, coming up with an idea. "Tell Sylvia, that got me Right Between the *Eyes*."

"Yes!" Monica shrieks, exited. "Yes, that's a great one."

"By Garbage," I say.

"*Right Between the Eyes*, by Garbage, Sylvia. Write that down."

I got one. That makes me not as nervous, but I can't think of any more.

"Ooh, ooh, ooh," Monica says. They are both giggling beyond control. I know I'm not that funny, and it's kind of cool, but it's also kind of difficult to do what I have to do. But listening to them both laughing together is pretty awesome. "*Behind Blue Eyes*, not the old one, the Limp Bizkit version. Yes!"

"That's a good one," I say. I'm actually very impressed.

"Sylvia wants to know," Monica says, but she can't really get a word out because they are both cracking up. I wish I could laugh like that instead of thinking all the time. Thinking is a disease infesting my brain cells, like, constantly. Finally Monica stops cackling long enough to say, "If, if behind Kelly Clarkson's hazel eyes, are really Limp Bizkit blue eyes?"

"What?" That doesn't even make sense, but for some reason, it's funny?

They are cracking up beyond return. I almost want to hang up and try again, you know, maybe later when she's by herself. But you never know when somebody is going to have her sister around. I wish Monica's sister were at Girl Scouts.

Then, suddenly, they both stop laughing on a dime. "Crap, they're calling us for dinner, Larry," Monica says. Which I guess is hilarious because they crack up again.

"What's so funny about dinner?" I ask, not meaning to sound annoyed.

"Sylvia said, 'Good, 'cause she's hungry like the wolf.' You're so lame, Sylvia. Now go. Tell them I'll be down in a minute. I'm sorry, Larry."

"It's okay. I thought you guys would have already been done with dinner."

"We're late eaters. My dad doesn't come home from work until after 7:00 and my mom wants us all to eat together."

"My mom does the same with us. I mean, with dinner. I mean, as a family. But tonight my sister is at Girl Scouts, so. . .I mean, sort of. "

"It was good talking to you," she says. "But I gotta go."

"Wait," I say with way too much urgency. Then softer I say, "Oh. It's okay."

"No, what?"

"I mean, tomorrow we have to do square dancing, you know?"

"Yeah. That'll be fun. Sort of. Maybe. Not."

I hear a somewhat murmured call for Monica and then she covers the phone, and calls back that she'll be right there.

"Oh crap, Larry, I gotta go—I'm coming! See you tomorrow though, okay?"

"Okay," I say. "Bye."

"Thanks for calling," she says. "Bye."

The sound on the other end of the phone after Monica hangs up is sort of like listening to darkness. The deepest darkest darkness there is in the world.

I'm all bummed that I didn't ask her to dance with me tomorrow. Maybe I could have just blurted it out in between "eye" songs. . .but I didn't.

Another eye song that used to be on the radio all of the time hits me, *Green Eyes* by Coldplay. I heard it again at camp this summer; Danny had it on his iPod. I never really heard the words before, but when I was listening to it during rest hour, it reminded me of Sara Rothman, even though she has blue eyes and the song is called *Green Eyes*. I started to write her another letter and tell her about the song, even wrote some of the lyrics down, like, ". . .anyone who tried to deny you, must be out of their mind. . ." kind of thinking about if you maybe had a flat chest if you're a girl, or just small if you're a boy. And I wrote part of the chorus, ". . .I came here with a load and it feels so much lighter now that I met you. . ." because that's how I felt dancing with her at my bar mitzvah, like I had finally met her, and all of it. . .but then I didn't send the letter. I put her address and a stamp on it too. But just like the other 13 letters, I never sent it.

TATTOO SHOW-N-TELL #4. . .
DECEMBER INSTALLMENT

*T*his one here on my right shoulder. Yeah. Aquaman. I seen you all lookin' at it when you walk up the steps. I like super-heroes and I like water. Seemed like a good one to get.

Okay then, sit back, sit down, and sit up straight. Here we go.

Chapter Twenty-Five

As Monica's class approaches, Mr. Stack orders us to "bring it in." We all put our arms into the center of the circle like a sports team.

"On three, I want to hear. . .square dancing!" Mr. Stack coach-speaks. "Okay?! One! Two! Three!"

"Square dancing," we also say, not too enthusiastically. Kevin says it in a girl voice and most everybody laughs.

"C'mon, you ninnies! You can do better than that! ONE! TWO! THREE!"

"SQUARE DANCING!" Neck veins. Love it. And Mr. Stack's whole face is beet red. He calms down and says in a low roar, "Now, go get you a partner, MEN!"

I go. I see Monica and she's wearing her typical tight jeans. For this unit, we don't dress out in PE clothes, another indication of how un-PE square dancing is. But Monica is pretty delicious in her jeans. They look brand new, and she's looking around, like she's trying to find somebody. I hope it's me.

I tap her shoulder. "Monica?"

"Oh, hey, Larry," she says nervously. Not laughing her head off like last night at all. But maybe she's just stressed out about lame dancing in PE like me.

"You wanna be my partner?" I say, I think loud for her to hear me.

She smiles. And then looks over my head and says, "I'm sorry, Larry, but somebody already asked me."

My heart drops out of my chest, slides down my own loose-fitting jeans and onto the dirty PE floor. Everyone will be dancing on top of it.

"Oh," I say. I want to ask who. Who could have possibly gotten here before me? I'm waiting to see, but she ends my curiosity.

"Yeah, Kevin asked me in math class."

"Oh," trying not to show her how much she just obliterated me. Kevin?!!

Kevin walks up to her and says, "Ready?" He looks right at me, through me. "You best find you a partner, Ratner. We're square dancin' here."

"Oh," I say again. He smiles, laughs a little, and takes Monica to the other side of the dance floor. She tries not to laugh as she's being swooped away, but it's like Sylvia is in the room again coming up with eyeball tunes, and Monica can't help it. She kind of looks back at me and then she doesn't. She looks at Kevin.

I can't believe this. Can't believe my eyeballs.

CHAPTER TWENTY-SIX

"Larry?" Someone says, tapping me on the shoulder.

"Huh?" I'm still watching Monica and Kevin disappear into the pool of dancing people when I turn around.

It's Heather Highland, another girl from Hebrew school. She wears glasses and she's really tall. Like my head comes up to just-below-her-chin-tall. Actually, she plays on the volleyball team and runs cross-country in the spring. She invited me to her bat mitzvah, but I didn't go. I probably should have, but it just didn't sound like it'd be fun since I didn't really know Heather. Her invitation had volleyballs on it, which was cool.

"You wanna dance?" she asks me. I stare, surprised, and still shocked about Monica and Kevin. When I don't answer, Heather says, "I, I know we're supposed to wait for somebody to ask us, but that's sort of risky, so I thought—"

"Oh—I mean, yes," I say. "Okay."

So it goes without saying that we must look like we're from the circus, just standing next to each other. If you see Heather's face, behind her big glasses are big brown eyes (which immediately makes me think of the song, *Brown-EYED Girl*). What I'm trying to say is, for a really tall girl, she's not ugly. She's got sort of a big nose, but that never really bothers me. Like a small chest doesn't bother me either. A nose is a nose, you know? Unless there are giant boogers sticking out of it, what's the issue?

I look over but I can't see Monica and Kevin. I'm stupid because Heather sees me do this. "Oh, did you want to ask somebody else?" she asks me.

"What? No. No." I try to sound believable. I look up, and for the first time I catch her eyes through those big glasses. "No," I say again.

"Okay," she's says, softer, letting out a breath, almost like I spared her life.

Mr. Stack introduces a new girls' PE teacher, "This here's Ms. Thompson, a square dancing expert. AN EXPERT! Let's give it up for Ms. Thompson."

We clap. Heather is smiling and clapping with some gusto.

"Howdy, partners," Ms. Thompson says and we all sort of murmur. Heather says howdy back. I try not to be obvious, but I'm looking for Monica and Kevin again – I can't seem to help it – but I don't see them.

Mr. Stack yells, "She said, HOWDY PARTNERS!" Making me jump.

"Howdy partners!" The boys all scream. I hear Kevin's girl voice and Monica's giggle, the cute one from last night on the phone. They are to my left and it's okay for me to look because everyone laughs at Kevin again. Monica is so close to him she can smell his clothes. Damn.

"Okay!" Ms. Thompson says, excited too. "Let's get started then."

Heather takes off her shoes. Apparently, lots of girls take off their shoes to dance with me. She also takes off her glasses and puts them inside her shoes, "It'll be better this way," she sort of whispers, and I'm not sure what she means exactly.

"Oh," I say, my classic response to everything apparently.

Square dancing isn't sexy or anything and that's why they let you do it in school. You're supposed to hold each other's hands way out in front of your bodies and put your other hand on your partner's back, and when Heather puts her hand on my back it sort of surprises me. I'm telling you, we look like a circus act. Heather smiles though, and without those big thick glasses her face looks okay, sort of softer even. I mean, I'm not saying I'm some kind of Bruno Mars or Justin Timberlake either. I'm not saying that.

"You have to give me your other hand," Heather says to me as we do a one-step, two-step groove that Ms. Thompson shows us with Mr. Stack. Heather's hand is probably a normal girl hand, but it practically swallows mine. I'm not kidding; they make us all twirl our partners. Heather has to literally bend down to get under my arm. I think about apologizing for that, but I don't. She's breathing hard and laughing too. Girls have a good time at dances; they just do, even in PE.

"What are you doing your essay on?" she asks me, probably because I'm not talking or even looking her in the eyes like a good human being, and because we're in the same English class, so she's trying to fill the uncomfortable silence with *something* vs. nothing, which is exactly what I'm giving her.

Today, Mrs. Grammar Tree made us brainstorm what we're comparing and contrasting for our big essay so that's probably why she's bringing it up. One girl is going to compare and contrast dogs to cats. That's kind of lame. One guy wants to compare and contrast Snickers bars to Milky Ways. Now that's a good topic.

"I don't know," I say. Which is true, but I feel bad because I know she's just trying to have a conversation with me and I'm one utterance and out.

"Me neither," she says. "I was thinking of comparing and contrasting being a kid from a divorced family versus a family with both parents, but then I thought maybe comparing kids who wear glasses to kids who have braces to kids who have glasses *and* braces, but then I should just compare cereals, you know, cereals that talk, like Rice Krispies, to cereals that have prizes in them, like, Lucky Charms." She finally takes a breath. "So, no, I haven't decided yet."

"Those are good," I say, staring down at Heather's big feet in her white socks, but then catching Monica and Kevin prance by us. Me and Heather do-si-do. Please don't ask me to explain that stupid move, but Monica and Kevin are pros at it. Ms. Thompson picks them to show everybody: The model do-si-do-ers.

Maybe I should compare and contrast superheroes, like Superman to Aquaman. I'm thinking about this as Kevin and Monica, in her *super* tight jeans, model a reverse do-si-do maneuver where the boy is actually twirled by the girl, and I'm the only one who doesn't have to bend to fit under the girl's arm.

Superman and Aquaman are classic Super Friends who fight bad guys, but I think they are both really lonely too. Fighting bad guys and doing the right thing constantly is not something everybody can just do. Superman is on Earth alone, and even if he wants to tell Lois Lane everything, he really can't. He can't tell anyone his secrets; so everybody loves him, but nobody really knows him.

I'm saying none of this to Heather.

Just feeling lousy because every time I think I'm going to say something to her, anything even, I see Monica and Kevin twirling or do-si-do-ing in front of us, just smiling and laughing. I want to stop staring but my body won't let me.

I think about telling Heather I'd rather be Aquaman than Superman, but I don't. "Serious, those are good topics," I just say, not looking anywhere near her eyes.

"Okay?" she says, slightly irritated I think, wanting me to keep talking probably.

The thing is, Aquaman goes under water and it's all peaceful, but when he comes to the surface, right away the noise of Metropolis or whatever the city is, kind of hurts his ears. Sometimes, I wish I could live under water, like him. . .

I'm probably in a big trance, not saying any of this out loud, and at the same time, with my own superhero peripheral vision, I see Monica and Kevin look over at us, and somewhere in all of my hazy moments, I realize I'm not even moving anymore. Suddenly I look up at Heather, staring at me, and say, "Oh. I'm sorry, I stopped dancing—"

"It's okay." Heather cuts me off, almost too loud because she sees me see them, sort of tugs at me like a remote control that you smack because it's low on battery power, and we're square dancing again. "C'mon," she says, twirling and leading me at the same time to the other side of the floor, glaring at Monica.

"Maybe superheroes," I say, trailing behind her.

"What?"

"I may do my essay on superheroes, but, but probably not. I don't know."

I want to tell her how all Aquaman's friends are different shapes and sizes, some with big noses like a hammerhead shark, and some with no noses like a jellyfish, and when you're under water, like that's your home, nobody cares what anybody looks like or swims like or how big the bubbles are that come out of their mouths. Nobody is just short like me. But then I think that's too stupid to say out loud, and that Kevin will show up as soon as I say anything and snap me in the back with a towel right in the middle of me and Heather dancing, and maybe that's why I can't stop looking at them.

Heather sees me staring again. She yanks me into a do-si-do, and all amped, says, "Wasn't your bar mitzvah the best day you've ever had in your whole life?"

For some reason, this question startles me. I stop looking for Kevin and Monica for a second and I think I'm staring instead at Heather's boobs because that's just where my eyes come to. She really has me stumped, "I don't know," I say.

In the middle of a reverse do-si-do, mid-twirl, Heather lets go of my hand and I stumble and fall. That's right, I take a spill in PE from square dancing. When I catch my balance and look up at Heather, her arms are crossed in front of her chest. She's already got her shoes and her glasses back on.

"I'm sorry you had to dance with me instead of—" She cuts herself off like she might get too angry if she finishes her sentence, and too loud. For the first time today, I'm riveted to only her now, not watching for anything else, wanting to get up, but stuck, and wanting to say something, anything, like, *no, it's okay, I didn't mean to stare at Monica and Kevin. . .* but nothing comes out of my mouth.

Now she's the one staring at Monica and Kevin. She stares and stares and while staring, she says really loud, "My bat mitzvah was the best day ever." She's angry and everyone is looking at us, I swear. But then from the deepest part of the back of her throat, she says, "Sorry you weren't there – clearly you had other plans," in the sweetest, softest, saddest, totally not angry way. It's like all of it just transferred from the back of her throat to mine, and totally crushes my whole esophagus. My brain is telling me to reach for her – in front of everyone, it doesn't matter – hug her even, keep her forever; that's how quick it all happens. But my body doesn't do anything. Like my crushed throat, the rest of me is frozen, stuck, broken.

Then Heather just leaves – in the middle of our do-si-do, in the middle of the song, in the middle of our dance, the middle of PE. The southern dude in the music is saying, *swing your partner 'round and 'round,* but I no longer have one. Heather walks up to Ms. Thompson, gets a pass or something, and she's gone in three steps, and I'm alone in the middle of the dance floor. Serious.

CHAPTER TWENTY-SEVEN

To top off a day of 100% suckage, now I have to take the bus home. I consider just walking home even though it's seven miles away and it would take me until it's past dark to get there. It might be worth it.

But like a nasty habit, I get on the bus. I'm about to sit down in a middle seat when I hear Robert Bullock's, "Hey Ratner! Hey, Raaatner!" coming from the steps, waiting to get on the bus. Even though the bus driver also hears Bullock bellowing my name, he just looks back down at his bus driver chart. Devon is behind Robert calling my name too, and now it's in stereo, the whole time up the steps with, "Hey Ratner! Hey Raaaaaat! Ratner!" Over and over. I want to move, but there are too many open seats around me, and Robert and Devon are locked in, all hyper as they sit down next to me. They're so loud – pretty much the whole bus is looking at me. I'm trapped. Stuck.

The bus starts to move, doing the typical slow-roll out of the parking lot, waiting for the 40 million buses in front of us to go. Right about now, I wish I were at Cherry Hill Mall trying on winter clothes and counting to infinity.

Robert and Devon stand, and a bunch of their friends gather around behind me.

"Now, Ratner," Robert says. "Devon here says you called him a fag."

"What?" I say. "I didn't say jack about him."

"It's what he said you said. He said he didn't like your ex-girlfriend Sara Rothman because she was a little vacant in the ta-ta department and you got mad and called him a derogatory term for homosexual." The whole time Devon is standing, just staring at me and occasionally smiling, but mostly, he's trying to look wild and mean. "You callin' Devon here a liar?"

"I didn't say anything," I turn away and look out the window. Robert pushes over even more. Devon is just standing there, hovering.

"Devon, Ratner here says he never called you a fag."

Devon punches me in my arm. "That's what you get for calling me a liar," and then laughs and gives Robert a high five.

"Don't call my friends liars, Ratner." And he punches me in the arm. Not too hard, even softer than Devon's.

"Quit it, okay? Just quit it!"

"Or what?" Devon asks and he gets in my face, all serious.

"Or he'll go to the principal again," Robert says.

Devon hits me in the same spot and says, "That's what you get for going to the principal on my friend here."

Looks like my mom called my sensei *and* the principal even though I told her not to. "I didn't go to the principal," I say, covering my arm with my other hand.

"Are you calling my friend here a liar?" Devon asks me. "'Cause the principal called him into his office today."

"Well, I didn't say anything to him."

They both hit me again.

"Quit it!" I scream. "I didn't call him a fag or go to the principal! Just quit it!"

"What's going on back there?" The bus stops at Robert Bullock and Devon's stop, and the bus driver looks in the rear view mirror. "Hey! Break it up!"

They both stand. Robert leans over, gets right in my face, and says softly, "You go to the bus driver too, Ratner?" And flicks my ear discreetly as he grabs his backpack.

"Well, you know he went to his mommy," Devon spits. He looks at me, "You gonna lie about that too, Raat-ner? Thought Jews weren't supposed to lie?"

"Since Ratner is the shortest Jew ever, he gets a handicap," Robert says.

As Devon reaches behind to put his backpack on, he elbows me hard in the arm, the same spot both of them punched me. Again, the bus driver can't see it and I'm not about to point it out to him.

They both leave, finally, laughing and high-fiving each other and chanting, "Hey, Ratner!" one after the other like cartoon hyenas. The bus finally pulls away, but I can still see them repeating, "Hey, Ratner," when I look out the window.

My sensei says to control my anger, but maybe that's not always the right thing to do. Just seems like I never really know what to do. I keep thinking that I don't want to be like my mom and go nuts over every little thing. Except for the temper part, I've always thought I was more like my dad, but I don't know anymore. All I do know is I wish I could shut my brain off for good.

CHAPTER TWENTY-EIGHT

We're on our way to the old neighborhood, back to Douglass Turn, my old street. Just me and my parents, who are meeting up with our old neighbors to "do the lunch thing." After yesterday, the only good news is it's the weekend.

I didn't have to go with my parents back to the old neighborhood; I wanted to go. I think if you think about a place long enough, you gotta go there. Plus I want to get the heck out of Cherry Hill and Robert Bullock and Devon and Kevin and Monica and Heather and square-frickin' - dancing, even for a couple of hours at least. But I don't say that to my parents, because then they'll get on the phone again to the principal and my sensei and the bus driver and the whole world and make my life even worse. If that's possible. Which it isn't.

So when my dad asks me why I want to come back to the old neighborhood, I have to think fast. "I want to go by Jack's house," I say. Which I kind of do because I'd been thinking about the whole Jack thing since my bar mitzvah, when we saved a spot for him, but Kevin drank his iced tea.

I know Douglass Turn won't be the same because we were the last to move out of the neighborhood, and even though Jack won't be there, I want to go to his house anyway.

"How come?" my dad asks me, squinting in the rear-view, confused.

"I don't know," I say.

He looks at my mom and then puts his serious-type voice in his throat and says, "Hey, Larry, you know Jack's mom parked that car around the block and I'm pretty sure it's still there." Then to my mom he asks, "What was that car, a Buick?"

"It wasn't a Buick," my mom says as if the whole world is stupid because the car that used to be in Jack's driveway isn't a Buick.

"Well, what? A Dodge? Couldn't have been a Dodge."

"I can tell you one thing, it wasn't a Dodge," my mom says. She's sure of everything the car isn't.

"I think it was a Buick—"

"It was just a hatchback," I say. Because it was. "A white hatchback. That's all."

For some reason, they both don't say anything until my dad finally goes, "Right. That's right. A hatchback. Well, anyway, I heard Mr. Scolden tried to buy it from her last year, but she wouldn't sell it."

"Oh. That sucks," I say. Because it does suck.

Yeah, this is the car ride up. My stomach feels like they are running those psycho tests where they make the mice run through mazes.

Me and Jack were the last ones to leave the neighborhood. I feel lousy because it wasn't like we traded phone numbers when my other friends moved away from Douglas Turn. Everybody left and nobody said, like, "Here's my new phone number. Call me." One day their parents told them they were moving, and now this whole block, the best block there ever was in America, is over.

It was about the time when everyone had moved away—Bobby, Jaime, and this other tall kid our age, Adam—that I really got to know Jack McCaffery.

Jack looked like a homeless guy who needed a shower and a good dog maybe. He was pretty tall for his age, which of course means he was way taller than me. He always slouched, though, like he was hungry or something. He would wear the same t-shirt and corduroy pants all the time, even in the summer, like Shaggy from Scooby–Do.

Jack's parents were divorced. I know people get divorced left and right in the world, but he was the only guy I ever really knew who lived with just one parent.

"My mom has a boyfriend who is around a lot," Jack would say. He always had a blade of grass in his pocket that he'd stick in his mouth when he was nervous, which was most of the time.

"What? Does he tell you what to do and stuff?"

"He walks around upstairs naked like it's nothing."

Jack could always crack me up like that.

He also taught me how to play the board game Risk, and we'd play at least twice a week at his house. Risk is the best game in the world; jeez, it's got the whole world *in* the game. Serious – every continent and country on earth is on the board, and you have to strategically conquer all the continents until you rule the world. I never won. Jack always ruled the world and that's the truth. Thinking about it now, I know some teacher probably made the whole game up so jerky kids like us would learn some geography.

Jack told me once, "Larry, when I die, I'm leavin' this Risk game to you."

"Cool." I could play Risk forever and never fall asleep. And I know it's stupid, but I wish all that stuff we're learning about WWII could have been a giant game of Risk instead of an actual war. Like all these rulers sit at a huge table, even Hitler, and play the game. Or even the stuff in Israel now, where Sara's family is. Sara, her dad, and me and a

Palestinian or two could work the whole deal out with two games of Risk. Serious.

Jack's mom was hardly home. She had a job as a telephone operator for 911 calls that kept her away from the house a lot. She didn't chew on a piece of grass, but she was nervous too, just like Jack. And she squinted when she was listening or thinking maybe. Marna's a squinter too.

Jack's mom would come home from work at night, all tired, and she'd bark orders at Jack. She would spend time with her boyfriend because he worked the graveyard shift. I mean, I don't think she knew Jack like I did. I don't think she knew him too well at all.

Mostly, Jack did whatever he wanted to do because no one was around to tell him not to. One of the things he did was read a lot. I guess he read *The Outsiders* when we were in the 6th grade on his own, because he'd always quote stuff from it, calling me "Ponyboy" like I knew what that was all about.

"Stay gold, Ponyboy," he'd tell me.

"Who's Ponyboy?"

And maybe that's why I've been thinking about the whole thing so much, because we just finished *The Outsiders* in my reading class. It's the first book I'm actually going to read again. I brought it with me for the car ride, thinking I could read some over the bridge or something, but now I'm too nervous to read.

Chapter Twenty-Nine

I guess I should probably say that Jack died when we were in 6th grade.

So, yeah. Sucks. That's why he wasn't at my bar mitzvah.

Jack was playing outside, by himself, after dinner. Like usual. I remember because the next day was track and field day at school. Jack had asked me if I could play, but my parents never let me play outside after dinner. I hate that, still. Anyway, the story goes Jack was playing inside his mom's car, the white hatchback.

"Dad, what happened last night?" I remember asking on the way home from dinner the next day. "Was there a fire or something? I heard sirens."

"No, there was an accident, not a fire." My mom was there and she gave my dad one of those mom looks, and then my dad said, "Actually, Jack got hurt." He was talking real slow, and he wouldn't look at me in the rearview.

"Jack's a tough kid, Dad. People don't think he's a tough kid, but he is. Somebody's gonna find that out the hard way some day."

"Yeah, he's a tough kid," with no oomph to it, like it's the saddest thought.

"So, he got hurt?" I asked, fidgeting in the back seat. "He break something? Is he home yet? He wasn't at school today. He missed his event."

My dad's face seemed like it got older or something. Maybe I asked too many questions at the same time. I can do that without knowing I'm doing it.

"No, Lar." We were at a stop sign, stopped, and my dad finally looked in the rearview at me. "Jack died on the way to the hospital."

"Oh." I didn't know what to say. Nobody taught you what you were supposed to say when your friend dies. So I just said, "oh" again.

My mom blurted in like she was Socrates or something. "See? Don't ever, *ever*, play with the emergency brake. A car is not a toy. It's a weapon!"

With my mom, there's always gotta be a lesson. So, here's what I got – if you hit the emergency brake in your parents' car, don't run behind the car to try and stop it. Like Jack did. You'll still get in tractor-loads of trouble, but you won't be dead, and that's supposed to be healthier for you.

"Best thing you can do is pray for him every night," my dad said.

"How?" I asked. I mean, praying for people always sounds kind of silly to me. I recited prayers for my bar mitzvah, but I didn't really think doing those prayers to or for Jack would be appropriate, or make any kind of difference. Plus, I was kind of shocked, maybe in denial, until all that eventually wore off, and I just felt lousy about Jack.

My dad is a master at making things simple. "Just talk to him," he said, and shrugged his shoulders like he was stumped.

My mom looked at me in the mirror on her visor flap and said, "When Pop Pop died, it was a shock too." Her father died when I was four from a sudden heart attack.

"And you pray for him every night?" I asked.

"I was having difficulty dealing with going from 100 to zero just like that. My dad was there and then he wasn't. So, at night, I'd imagine having a conversation with him and what he would say back to me. Especially when I'd get sad about him being gone. I think that's what your father means."

My dad nods, opens his mouth, but then doesn't say anything.

Anyway, I've tried to talk to Jack, but it doesn't really work. I can't imagine him talking back to me. Maybe my imagination is broken. I still try though.

But sometimes, when I try and talk to him, I kind of get pissed at him even though I don't mean to. Then I feel guilty for getting pissed at a dead guy, and then I get pissed at myself for thinking too much, like I always do. And then, and this is the worst part, especially when it's all dark in my room and I'm trying to pray to my dead friend before I go to bed: I get really lonely. Because Jack was the smartest kid I've ever met – straight As and everything – but he was way smarter than straight As. And we always knew we were alike because he thought too much too, like me. But then I think about what happened to him. . .and at least on that day, that moment, he didn't think at all. Who tries to stop a rolling car with their body? It's stupid. And thinking about that still wrecks me.

The day after Jack died, our teacher, Mr. Marciano, took us to the backstage of our school's theatre, the whole class, and had us sit down in a circle, holding hands. My mom says Mr. Marciano is Italian. She knows by the guy's mustache I guess, but she knows. All I know is that he's the hairiest teacher I've ever had. Then, I couldn't believe it, we're all backstage and he just starts crying like a baby in front of the whole class. And not just quiet tears slowly rolling down his face. He was bawling out loud, his entire body heaving up and down, full-out crying. Then the whole class starts crying with him. I didn't. I just took my hands back and put my head in 'em, because I don't cry; I just couldn't. Mr. Marciano really liked Jack. He took the time to understand him, that's for sure. Sitting there backstage, holding hands, was the first time I've ever seen a grown man cry.

CHAPTER THIRTY

My hand hurts when I knock on the door. Jack has one of those metal doors, not a wood door, that hurts when you knock on it in the winter. There's a picture of Santa Claus riding Rudolph taped right above the handle. I'm standing here thinking Santa Claus has no business being on a reindeer that small.

I knock again. Forty years go by, I swear, before his mom answers.

"Larry?" She has a tissue in her hand and reaches up to wipe her nose. Her eyes look like she's been rubbing them; her eyes always looked that way.

"What brings you by the neighborhood, Larry?" She asks. She's surprised, probably because I didn't call first like my mom suggested I do. I didn't want Mrs. McCaffery sitting around thinking about what I want; especially when I didn't and still don't even know myself.

I watch Mrs. McCaffery turn her head away, wrap her Kleenex around her pointer finger like it's a finger glove, and rub her right nostril hard. See, when you're older or a mother, you can get away with picking at your nostril like that, but not at my age.

"Hi, Mrs. McCaffery." I don't really look up at her, so she probably doesn't even hear me. I'm just staring at her toes coming out over her slippers. She has some pink nail polish on them, but it's chipping like Marna's always do.

"You want to come in, Larry? I think we have some pop. You want some pop?"

"Okay." Jack always had soda, but he called soda, "pop," just like his mother.

Mrs. McCaffery disappears into the kitchen while I stand in their living room. I think this is the living room that I'm in now. I don't know.

There's no TV, just a yellow couch with the plastic still on it and a light green chair that you can pull down the lever so you can lay down. But it's the kind of chair that you need to have a TV so you can pull the lever to kick back and operate the remote control like you're the king of the living room.

Honestly, I don't want to sit down on either piece of furniture. I don't want to sit down. I pretty much want to drink my pop standing up.

Mrs. McCaffery comes in with a glass of root beer for me, with one of those crazy straws that look like Marna's hair after it rains.

"Why don't you sit down, Larry." Okay, so I sit in the green chair, but I don't touch the lever. Mrs. McCaffery sits down on the plastic-covered couch and crosses her legs like women do. She doesn't smile; she just crosses her legs and ties her bathrobe tighter. "So Larry, what brings you—"

"Jack said I could have his Risk game—maybe he mentioned it to you?"

"No, huh-uh." She says, fidgeting with the belt on her robe for no real reason. "He never mentioned it."

"Oh, well, he maybe said it to me like a joke. That I could have it if he didn't. . .I mean if he didn't need it anymore."

"I'm sorry, you should have told me sooner, Larry, or, or called. We gave all of Jack's stuff away, you know shortly after—"

"Oh, no, that's okay. It was just something I thought of, ah, just today." And with that I downed the whole glass of root beer in one gulp. Screw the straw.

Mrs. McCaffery looks up at me and taps her nose with the tissue. I have to pee. I've got kidneys that never quit.

"Do you want another pop?"

"No thanks."

She takes my glass and then I hear that rusty faucet squeak from the kitchen. It always sounded like the whole sink wall shook before even a drop came out of the spigot.

"I'm sorry I couldn't make your bar mitzvah," Mrs. McCaffery says from the kitchen. "Congratulations though, Larry. A man now, huh?"

Man, Mrs. McCaffery blows her nose about 12 times before I say, "I. . . I'm not really good at saying stuff."

She pats her left nostril as she returns from the kitchen, and then tries to sniff and breathe through her nose like she's got a million allergies or something. Finally she says, "Okay. Take your time. What did you want to say—"

"I just get confused," I say, interrupting, kind of snapping at her. "And I can't stop thinking about it. 'Cause he's smarter—was smarter than that."

I can tell Mrs. McCaffery is trying to be nice, but I think I'm really starting to aggravate her and she's regretting inviting me in for pop. "Maybe he just didn't think, Larry, you ever consider that?" Everything feels rotten right here, right now. The only thing that feels okay is Mrs. McCaffery knows exactly what I'm talking about; I don't have to spell it all out. I don't have to ask what the hell was Jack *thinking*

when he tried to stop a rolling car from moving. It makes
zero sense.

"No," I say, way too loud. "No way. He was too smart—"

"He wasn't that day—"

"No, no! People don't just change in one moment
like that—"

"He got scared, Larry!" Mrs. McCaffery yells. Her eyes
are bulging at me right now. If she were a monster, she'd
probably just eat me in one gulp. She takes a breath, a big
sigh, like my mom sometimes does when she's trying not
to be aggravated. "Okay?" She asks, softly. "That day. That
moment. He got scared and didn't think. Period."

I shake my head, no way. "Didn't seemed scared of bein'
run over."

"I said he didn't think, Larry. Listen," she says, pleading
with me. "He was scared of getting in trouble with. . ." But
she can't finish the sentence.

Mrs. McCaffery keeps pulling her bathrobe belt tighter. If
she pulls it anymore, she'll literally saw herself in half. Seriously.

Then it all hits me and it's so sad, too sad. Because when
I get scared, I do the exact opposite – I sit there on the bus
and think and think and think, and do nothing. At least
Jack did something, and doing *something* and dying has got
to be better than doing nothing and barely living. I don't
know. . . I don't even know if I believe that.

"Jack was my son—I knew him. He was your friend,
Larry, but he was my son. I know I didn't get to spend as
much time. . .like how most mothers—"

"Yeah, yeah, that's it." I almost stand up, but then I don't.
"See, that's it."

"That's what?" she snaps. Again, I'm back to irritating
Mrs. McCaffery.

"I did spend time with him a lot, you know, and I think maybe I should, or maybe I could tell you some stuff I know. . .maybe."

She looks down at her slippers and then she brings her right leg up to her chest. She starts pickin' at her big toe. She's pickin' at the polish.

"I found out a lot of things after he. . .well, you know after he died," she says. "I can say *died* can't I?"

"It's just too bad you didn't know before he—you know, ah, before." I'm actually trying to say something good for Jack's mom, but it comes out all mangled instead.

But Mrs. McCaffery is a tough lady; she lets out a breath like she's been holding extra in her lungs for about a year. And then she sort of smiles.

"Wow. You didn't come here to make me feel awful now did you?"

She stands up and starts to take the plastic off the yellow couch. Why is she deciding to remove the plastic today, right now? I stand up too, but I don't feel any better, especially because I think I said something to Jack's mom that I didn't really mean, because I can never say stuff the way I actually mean it.

"Oh, no, no, no—"

"It's about time I take this ugly plastic off," Mrs. McCaffery says as she swipes at the cover, swinging it over my head with one big swoop. "I usually take it off when we have guests, but we haven't had guests in a long time—you're a guest, Larry. It's about time I take this ugly plastic off for good, right? Things can't stay clean forever."

She's sniffing up a storm now, as if I blew a whole dust cloud up her nose, but she holsters the tissue back in her bathrobe belt like a weapon.

"I like it either way. On or off. It's a nice couch, Mrs. McCaffery. Yellow."

"I loved Jack, Larry." She looks right at me for a second and then back to the plastic in her hands as she attempts to fold it all up. "And I'm going to regret my whole—well, I have regrets you know. Here, take an end."

I sort of fumble it before I grab a chunk of plastic in each hand. "See, I think that's—I mean, just—I mean, he told me that when you would laugh or, you know, be chill, he loved, you know, bein' home. I don't know."

Mrs. McCaffery starts to cry right as I'm talking. I swear.

She makes me so nervous crying, trying to wipe it up with that tissue that I start to cry too. I know I don't cry, but I think right here's where I'm breaking my own rule.

"Ugh, Larry," she says with a big-time sigh. "You're too much."

"I miss him, Mrs. McCaffery." That slipped out. I knew I didn't want to tell Jack's mother that I miss her son. The son that died. I look around the room trying to find a Kleenex box. There must be a million of those boxes in this house. Or does she produce tissues internally like cells?

"I miss him too, Larry." She's crying and trying to smile at the same time, just like an actress. She's all over her face with that tissue.

Then she walks towards me and puts the back of her hand right on my cheek.

"He said those things?" I nod. "About me?" I nod. "Really?" I nod.

She's scaring the crud outta me. I should leave. Jack would have. . .slid right under his mom's arm and out the door so fast you'd think he escaped through the crack at the bottom of the door. And Mrs. McCaffery would call his name, let out a sigh, light up a cigarette maybe, then go back inside – leaving the door open just a tad because Jack never carried a key. We'd hear Mrs. McCaffery call for him one more time. It kind of echoed in the cul-de-sac on Douglass Turn. The old neighborhood.

"He was a golden kid," she says to me now, after dropping the folded plastic cover on the yellow couch.

And then she gives me one of those mother hugs, only stronger, for about two hours.

CHAPTER THIRTY-ONE

The hatchback door is unlocked. More like broken. I open the hatch, climb in, and there it is – the emergency brake. The WEAPON. If I touch it, will it slice me right open? I can hear my mom saying not to lick the cream cheese off the knife: "You'll cut your whole tongue off." It's sort of like that.

I don't know what made me come here. Walking down Mrs. McCaffery's driveway, I started feeling sorry for the white hatchback – banished to the back of the street, hibernating like a big fat bear for the last two years since Jack died.

I touch the radio, just above the emergency break. There's a small two-inch crack in the windshield, and I think, yup, this kind of car should have a crack like that in the windshield. And if it didn't, I would put one there. Now that I'm inside the car, it smells like a carnival – a mixture of cotton candy, cigars, and something else really old and wet.

I touch the emergency brake fast like it's on fire or something, just to be sure it's not loose or that the car won't roll; and if it starts to roll, I'll just get out and watch it roll and roll and roll and so what? They won't find me dead underneath this hatchback.

That's the thought that sends me into like a deep type of slumber. Maybe it's the carnival smell or Mrs. McCaffery, or the whole cul-de-sac, but whatever it is, all of a sudden I'm very sleepy. I never take naps, but man, I can't hang on.

I guess I climbed into the hatch part of the hatchback, and blammo – out like a light. I was dreaming, I know. 'Cause if you're in the thick of a dream and you wake up, you remember every dang piece of it.

So I was dreaming I was going down this river, backward, without a boat. I kept trying to turn around forward, but I couldn't. The river was no deeper than a puddle, but it was filled with all kinds of gross things; I was rolling on top of blood and guts (yes, real guts) and brains and hearts and legs and arms and hairs and here's the weirdest part: I'm rolling on top of smiles too. Yeah, like smiles of the people I know – Marna, Mom and Dad, kids from the old neighborhood, and Mr. Marciano backstage at the theatre, and Mrs. McCaffery with a cigarette, and Jack with a blade of grass, Monica Johnson in her jeans, Heather's eyes after she takes off her glasses, and even Sara Rothman – not in her dress though – in Israeli army digs holding a giant rifle that's too heavy for her. Smiling.

Somebody needs to paint what's in my head when I'm dreaming and give me half the profits from the pictures they sell. Serious.

My dad wakes me up when he opens the hatchback door. I spring up and jump out instantly. My heart is popping like a someone threw a dozen snap-its at my chest, and I'm looking at my dad's face to see the same smile that was in my dream. It occurs to me that it's dark, hearing-crickets-type of dark, and it's cold, and my whole dream is swimming around in my brain before anybody starts talking.

My mom grabs and hugs me. That's two giant mother hugs in one day.

Then she lets go, motions all of us to move away from the hatchback (before it eats us alive!), and looks at my dad. He sighs, gets his keys out of his pocket and says, "Boy. . .you just might be grounded." My mother begins crying and walking at the same time, and says let's go home. And so we do.

CHAPTER THIRTY-TWO

"Do you know why you're here?" the man with the beard asks me. The truth is that I don't even know where I am. We left the house and my parents said for me to come with them. But it's weird 'cause before we leave, Marna says, "I'll stay here."

"You stay here," my dad says.

"I'll stay here," Marna says again.

"No need for you to come," my mom says, like they rehearsed it. "Stay here."

"Okay," Marna says.

Huh?

"Can I stay here?" I ask.

"You come with us," my mom says. "I want you to come with us."

"You should come with us," my dad chimes in.

"For what? Where we goin'?"

"Just taking a ride. Gonna talk to somebody," he says.

"A ride would be good," my mom says.

I tell all this to the guy with the beard behind the big desk. He listens like he's trying to sniff me with his ears. When I finish telling him all the things that I do know about what I don't know, he just says, "You like football?"

"Football? Yeah. I mean, I don't play on a team or anything."

"But you like to throw it around some?"

I'm out in the parking lot of this place I don't know, throwing a football with this stranger. He unbuttons his shirt and I can't believe he just takes off his first shirt and throws the ball back and forth wearing dress shoes and slacks and just an undershirt.

"I'm like a sweat shop," he says. "Any time I move around, even in winter. I sweat like a dirty pig. But I love the game."

He's hairy; clumps of fuzz burst out of his undershirt, escaping up and landing on his chest, and that's probably why he's a sweaty dude. He reminds me of Mr. Marciano, but then Mr. Marchiano never took off his shirt, or asked me so many questions.

"So you like football?" He asks me again, winding his right arm round and round, loosening up like some kind of professional quarterback. I mean, c'mon, we're in a parking lot here.

"Yeah."

"What's your favorite sport?" He whips his arm across his chest, holding it with his other arm, groaning, as if all his arm bones hurt because he's warming it up.

"Why?" I ask. I'm not stretching, or moving, or talking more than I have to.

"Mine was baseball. Pitcher. But once I got to high school, I couldn't get anybody out anymore. So I started playing catcher." He slings his right arm behind his head to stretch. Big groan. "I like catcher because you can see the whole game, you know? It's a tough position, on the knees especially, but beautiful all at the same time, you know?"

I just say nothing because what for? Is this some kind of job where your parents take you to a random guy so he can play sports with you in parking lots?

"Your parents tell me you've got some things goin' on at school," he finally says.

"What?" I knew it. They sent me here. To what? Fix me? Because I'm broken?

"They're a little concerned about you."

I throw the ball hard without seeming like I'm throwing it mad or something. Perfect spiral. He catches it but shakes his hands as if I burnt holes through them.

"I guess my parents talk to everybody about me except for me."

He nods and asks, "And how does that make you feel?"

I don't answer. I'm tired of feeling and thinking about feeling. I just want to sleep. And dream. I can do that good. I throw the ball, softer this time.

"Basketball," I say.

He's about to throw the ball but stops when I say that. Then he smiles and his beard that's all wet and shiny from his pig sweat spreads all over his face.

"Basketball. Hmm. Why?"

"'Cause I like to show bigger dudes that they're not so big as they think they are. I'm writing a book called *101 Ways Not To Get Blocked When You're Not Even Five Feet Tall.* Are you some kind of a shrink?" That just popped out. It makes him laugh and then swallow the laugh when I say, "Well, are you?"

"I'd like to think we can make you bigger, not smaller. Right, Larry?" Then he steps forward and asks, "You don't want to get any smaller, do you?"

I can't believe it, just 'cause I fell asleep in a car? I mean we take road trips and they always try to get us to nap on the way. So I fell asleep in a car, just not *their* car. Big deal. Sue me. I just shut down and shut off. I'm so pissed at my parents. What? Was this part of my being grounded?

He throws the ball at me and I just let it hit my chest, like in that movie, *North Dallas Forty*, at the end when Nick Nolte just lets the ball hit his chest 'cause he's quitting football. I quit. I quit this shrink. I quit this family. I quit.

The shrink keeps talking though, now about Robert Bullock, but he doesn't know his name so he refers to him as the "young man" who "teases" me on the bus and I'm about ready to lose it again. I'm so pissed my parents brought me to a parking lot to talk to some hairy guy about what happens on the bus.

"It's okay if you're angry." Him saying that makes me angry. He's walking up to me I guess to get his football. I want to leave, run, but where would I go? I don't want to go home and I sure as heck don't want to get back in the car with my parents. I wish I could just go jump inside Jack's white hatchback again and sleep. Dream. I do.

"It's okay to be angry," he says again.

It feels like I'm back on the bus and everybody is looking at me and Robert Bullock is standing over me and he takes my backpack and passes it around the bus and he flicks my ear and puts his face into my face like he's gonna hit me and then laughs and laughs and laughs and everybody is laughing at me. Again. What happens is Robert Bullock can't just rag on me privately, he's gotta get his friends, Devon and John and Toby, to look. And then, somehow, they get every kid on the bus to stop thinking about the class they just left or about going home, or their PlayStation 4, or whatever it is that goes on in your head when you're riding the bus and waiting for your stop. . .Instead, everybody's staring AT ME. But I can't cry. Not on the bus. Then it's game over. I can't. Not here. No way.

"Are you angry, Larry?"

"No."

"Oh, c'mon. You're pissed, admit it."

"No."

"You hate me. I tricked you."

"I don't hate you. I don't even know you. And *you* didn't trick me."

"Okay, what do you hate?"

"Nothing. Everything. This parking lot. Your shirt, and, and. . ."

"I hate my shirt too, good, good, go. Keep going. What else?"

"Fine. I can't believe my parents would take me here."

"And what else?"

"Nothing."

"What else?"

"No."

He grabs my shoulders and turns me as he kneels down because he's big enough to be on one knee in the parking lot and still see me eye to eye. I ain't crying here for this guy. This shrink. This stranger.

He says, "Look at me." I'm screaming in my head no way, I ain't crying in no parking lot, no way. "Look at me," he says. I can't. "It's okay," he says in a whisper, "I know how you feel. And it's okay."

Just like with Mrs. McCaffery, but worse, I'm bawling. This guy is hugging me, saying, "There you go. There you go." Stuff my own dad doesn't do. But I can't help it. I'm a wreck, breaking my own rule, crying in a frickin' parking lot. I think my parents are hiding in some bush trying to spy, but I don't care 'cause I can't help it. I'm bawling and it's not just short tears either; it's making me feel sick and heave to where I can't breathe and he's just saying that it's okay over and over.

It takes forever, but once I calm down enough so I can breathe normal, I'm embarrassed to look at the guy. I'll be embarrassed to look at my parents too. Or anybody. A mirror even. He says, "I'm a psychologist, Larry, not a shrink. Your parents brought you to see me because they are worried you're having some problems at school. Fair. Now, I can't make you taller, but I can help get you *bigger*. And I'm sure as heck not gonna make you smaller."

I look down, away. I can't believe I was bawling in the damn parking lot.

"Here's what I know. You're my last appointment. And I'm not leaving tonight until we're done."

We go back to his office where he gives me a new box of Kleenex.

And then he gets me to tell him everything. This guy, Dr. Stone is his name, he just listens. I mean he talks too, mostly he asks me questions to get information, but it just feels different, like no pressure.

He tells me I'm normal even though I don't feel normal and it's normal to feel not-so-normal. He tells me that whatever I say in his office stays in his office, "Like a good, dependable friend," he says.

"Yeah, but my parents pay you."

"That's true," he says. "They pay me to help you. I don't have to be your friend. At all. . ." He flips through his legal pad and then stuffs it in his top desk drawer. Then he finds my eyes and says, "But I want to be," and extends his hand out for me to shake it.

I look at his hand and don't shake it.

But then I do. I don't know, I just shake his hand, and whatever. . .

CHAPTER THIRTY-THREE

I never get mail, but when we get home from the shrink's office, Marna opens the front door before we are even out of the car, which she never does. She never "greets" anybody because she is always upstairs in her room – whether there's a door attached or not – on the phone. She is holding an envelope and wearing a suspicious smirk on her face when she says, "Hi Larry. You got mail." I hold the envelope with two fingers, away from my body, in case it's a booby trap and Marna is really trying to blow me to smithereens. If I wasn't so fascinated by the return address, I would have focused on the looks between my sister and my parents regarding our little "secret" venture to the shrink's office, but instead, as I go up to my room, I'm staring at the curly writing and the stamped postage that look like hieroglyphics, but it's not; it's Hebrew.

Dear Larry,

It was sooooooo good to hear from you. We are still new here, so it's very lonely.

But today I went to my dad's work (I know, scary-dangerous, right?!), and I saw the giant WALL.

Did you know that you can play catch over that wall? I have dozens of boyfriends now who I've never seen.

Just kidding, you goofball. But I did play catch with some random Palestinians. That happened. I was looking up at the wall and a soccer ball came flying over. So I threw it back. Again, again, and again. Playing catch in the middle of a war - how cool is that?

I don't like to write, but I do like to draw. I'm including a picture I drew of an Israeli soldier sitting on post, petting a street kitten that he sort of adopted as his pet, as his partner, as he waits and waits and waits. He brings wet cat food and lets the kitten nibble it off the mouth of his gun. I like that.

I like you too.

Love,

Sara

P.S. I'm writing this from our bomb shelter. Not because there's been a siren and we have to go here, but because I like to come here and draw. I'm strange, I know. You can say it. My dad says I'm strange too.

OMG. I read the letter again. And again. And one time out loud to Snowball.

Marna swears up and down that she didn't touch any of my letters from the box, but I can never tell if and when Marna is lying or not. Plus she has that grin on her face, the same one she had when she was chomping down illegal Girl Scout cookies and almost died from a hive-infested allergic reaction. But I count the letters in the box and they all seem to be there, so. . . I don't even know.

All I do know is: Sara Rothman wrote me a letter. She said she likes me.

OMG.

CHAPTER THIRTY-FOUR

I write Sara Rothman back and tell her everything. I mean everything.

I tell her about Robert Bullock and what happens on the bus and how my parents want me to fight him back and get suspended from school, and how when I get suspended my parents will probably take me to Carvel for a big ice cream cake in celebration.

I tell her I'm seeing a shrink. Dr. Stone. I tell her about our parking lot sessions.

I tell her about Jackson McCaffery and seeing his mom, the Risk game, the plastic on the yellow couch, and falling asleep in the hatchback.

I tell her about the Girl Scout cookies; how my dad was going to whoop me but then didn't, and how Marna broke out in hives because she's in love.

I tell her I wished I lived in Israel too and that we went to same school and our seats would be next to each other again because of our last names and this time I would talk to her every day, and I would want to go to her bomb shelter with her after school and do my homework while she drew stuff.

I tell her my friends here still are not my friends, but...*she* is my friend. She was my friend even when we never talked to each other.

The last thing I tell her is I like her too, but I say that I more than like-like her. Then I say I think she's the most beautiful girl in the world. I include the WORLD because she's on the other side of it, so that's fair. I end with, LOVE Larry, and then I seal the letter and write BURN THIS over the flap. . .and put the letter next to all of the other letters I never had the guts to send Sara Rothman.

TATTOO SHOW-N-TELL #5...
JANUARY INSTALLMENT

Ah, pfff.
Nope. Not gonna do it.
Okay then, sit back, sit down, and sit up straight. Here we go.

The bus driver refused to deliver a Tattoo Show-N-Tell for this week because yesterday he had to mop up Harry Horton's urine. Apparently Harry told the bus driver that he drank ten white milks at lunch because he was dared to do so and he asked the bus driver to pull over. When the bus driver refused, Harry walked to the back of the bus, which is against the rules to stand up and walk in the aisle while the bus is moving. Everyone in the back of the bus got out of Harry's way, also against the rules because they were standing in the aisle. Harry proceeded to spray the little slice of floor behind the back seat, you know, under the great big red emergency lever, with his pee. Also against the rules.

CHAPTER THIRTY-FIVE

Needless to say, my mom is major stressed about the strike and losing both of their incomes, and therefore, so is my dad. I mean, I get it, but it doesn't mean they have to be so serious all of the time, always giving short, irritated responses when Marna and me utter any questions – like we're ruining the universe by talking. That's the atmosphere around here. They cut coupons every day now (used to just be Sundays) from the extra inserts that come with my route newspapers. And my parents bought all these comforters at wholesale cost at a warehouse so we start selling them at a huge flea market called English Town, an hour from our house. Apparently, this will be how we make ends meet during the teachers' strike; last year, we sold picture frames.

On flea market days – Saturdays and Sundays – my dad helps me with my newspaper deliveries by taking me out in the car so I get done faster. Then he and I head off to English Town all before the sun rises. We always stop at Dunkin' Donuts after my route before heading to English Town, and I get an orange juice and a big donut, usually a Boston Kreme. My dad brings in his huge Dunkin' Donut coffee mug with the monster handle and they fill it up with coffee for like a quarter. That's the kind of guy he is – a bear claw and big huge coffee kind of guy.

This year, there's no Dunkin' Donuts because we're on a tight budget. No bear claw. No Boston Kreme. My dad has his old DD mug filled with Ratner Instant Coffee and we both have two slices of buttered toast. Literally, homemade breakfast.

English Town is pretty cold this morning, and even though I'm in full snow gear, I'm still shivering. Usually the sun comes up and warms things a little, but it's overcast today, so there won't be any sun.

Between the steam in my dad's coffee and his breath, his glasses are all fogged up. He wipes them with his handkerchief like every five seconds and then blows his nose with the same handkerchief while we wait for people to come buy cheap comforters.

Last year when we'd do English Town, he was always in rare storytelling form, like somehow his tales were heat lamps warming us up. This year, not a peep.

I remember he'd get all proud and silly, going on and on about his glory days when he was a kid, playing baseball. But he wasn't lying; he can swing a mean stick. Last year he took me to his softball game in his old man league. My dad's team had the bases loaded in the last inning, two outs, down by two runs, and my dad was choosing his bat from the on-deck circle. I asked him, "Hey, are you gonna try and hit a grand slam?"

"Nope. Just gonna hit 'em where they ain't."

And he did. To the trees. The ball kept going off his bat until it just disappeared in the forest at the end of the outfield, like the trees ate the ball. Serious. Even though it took an hour for my dad to limp around the bases because of his bum knees and old-man belly, he was still a little man with loads of pop in his bat. I could never do that, just don't have the power. When I played Little League baseball, some-times I'd get a hit, but nothing that lit up the sky like big-ger kids. One time, I hit a ball that went through both the shortstop and left fielder's legs and rolled to the back fence. Even though it was easily a stand-up double caused by two errors, I slid hard into second base, so happy to be there, finally. Besides that day, I always felt like I disappointed him by not hitting a home run, or making any kind of all-star team. I wanted to, more than anything, but I've never been strong enough, or good enough, or tall enough, or at least as good as he was. Sometimes, it's really fun hearing about his all-star childhood, but other times I feel so guilty because I just want him to shut up. But today? I'd trade my winter coat for one morsel of a tidbit from the glory road that is my dad's childhood.

"I've been shooting," I say, because I can't take the silent treatment anymore.

He nods in mid-sip of his coffee, swallows and says, "That's good. Shooting is good." And it feels like the steam from his mug erases his whole face.

My parents finally took me off house arrest. So when I don't have karate, me and Snowball shoot in our drive-way. Snowball is not really a good rebounder, but he likes to chase the ball on the second or third bounce.

"500 a day," I say, trying to stifle the shivering in my voice. Trying to sound tough. "Like you told me."

He nods, but not really at me. More at the empty English Town street aisles in front of our set-up.

"Damn," he says, blowing on his cold hands again. "Where are the people?" We are getting zero traffic today at our Comforter Table, and even though I love hanging with my dad at English Town, if we come home empty, it won't be good.

On the way home, my dad pops open the glove compart-ment and retrieves a free-floating half a cigarette. I haven't seen my dad smoke since I was like five-years-old when he quit. Allegedly. A lighter magically appears in his hand as he rolls down the window an inch and lights up in one swoop-ing move, and smokes for the rest of the car ride.

CHAPTER THIRTY-SIX

When we get home, I see something I have never seen before: Marna is in the garage straddling a bicycle. Yeah, the one that has been hanging from the garage ceiling since, like, WWII. I always thought it was one of those antique things my mom likes to collect, but apparently, it's Marna's bike. And she's got knee and elbow pads, and a helmet, and well, she's ready to ride. I glance over at my dad and he glances back at me with the same look of surprise. Speechless. We're just not used to seeing Marna out of her room, let alone on a bicycle looking like some kind of action hero.

"Looks like you're ready to crash into things," my dad says, tapping her helmet, on the way into the house.

"Look, okay? You can just—you know?" my sister says.

Then I hear something I've never heard from Marna, "You want to go for a ride?"

"What?" I say, still way in shock.

"A ride. With me. Hurry up." She snaps her helmet strap on tight, pounds on her elbow and knee pads like she's about to get into a cage with a bear. She's ready to go!

I jump on my bike, which is always ready to go because I ride it just about every day. My sister's in a hurry, so she goes pretty fast for someone who never rides a bike or gets any exercise. Peddling behind her is surprisingly difficult.

"Where are we going?" I ask, huffing and puffing, barely within earshot.

"Just keep up, little brother."

We pedal past the Woodcrest Country Club where I sometimes sneak in and swim during the summer, and up Kressen Road, which is a main road, and enter another neighborhood. My sister knows exactly where she's going, a left on this street, a right on that street. I'm lost. I couldn't get back home if you paid me. Finally Marna stops in front of an apartment 2B.

I'm way out of breath, wheezing and coughing, about to launch a collection of mucus from the diaphragm, when Marna says, "This is it." I spit a pretty substantial phlegmy bomb to the curb. "Nice," she says.

"Where are we?" I gasp because I'm really trying to, ah, breathe.

She gets off her bike, removes her helmet and shakes out her hair. Then she sits on the curb in front of apartment 2B and says, "Look, okay? We're moving."

I pause and register what she's saying before I ask, "Again?"

"Yes. Again."

"How do you know?" I ask.

"What do you mean, *how do I know?* 'Cause I overhear. I eavesdrop. I spy. I'm a world-class spy. That's how. There are no secrets, Larry. The strike is killing them. The cold is killing them. Plus, ah, you. They are dying blah blah blah. Period. That's them."

The idea of moving away from my lousy Cherry Hill existence is really appealing to me. To never have to get on the bus again, or see Monica Johnson, or Kevin, or have to square dance. . .I'd move to the North Pole. At the same time, it's lousy to think we'd up and move just because I won't fight Robert Bullock.

"Where?" I ask. I point. "Here? Apartment, 2B?"

"West," she says, all stone-faced. "California's too expensive. So, Vegas, baby."

"Las Vegas?"

"You'll be going to school underneath the Golden Nugget Hotel and Casino," she says, kicking her bike tire. "Taking math classes like poker, blackjack, and craps."

"Las Vegas?" I ask again, trying to see my future high school in neon lights.

"It's a joke. Mom is so into making us live the Jewish life by the Jewish law, right? Ha. There's like 1% Jewish people in Las Vegas. Ah, hello? Baruch atah adonai, we've got a winner!"

It's kind of funny listening to my sister. She's the only person who gets funnier the angrier she becomes. But then she gets all serious and it scares the crud outta me.

"This is Bucky's apartment. I love him and he loves me." She fidgets with her gears, then smacks her handlebars hard and sighs, annoyed. "Whoever heard of moving across the country when you've got a kid in high school? Whoever heard of that?"

Neither of us moves or says anything; we just stare at the 2B on the door.

Her eyes and whole body are sort of freaking me out. "So, what? You're gonna live with Bucky?"

"Hey," she calls at me, making me look at her. "Wouldn't you go to Israel and be with that girl if you could? With Sara?"

I want to say, hell yes I would, that I'd go in an Israeli minute if I could, but who am I kidding? "I'm 13, Marna. I can't even get into R-rated movies, let alone shack up with Sara Rothman in Israel—"

"But *if* you could. If age didn't matter, 'cause when you love somebody, you don't sit around thinking about how old you are or how old they are—"

"If, if, if, if," I say, getting frustrated. Maybe because she's making me think about something I don't want to consider. It hurts to think about Sara Rothman all the way over in Israel, huddled in a bomb shelter, drawing pictures of soldiers and cats, and thinking about all the things I should have said to her when we sat next to each other for 180 days. "If. . ." I say softer to my sister, with no umph to it.

Maybe I fell in love with Sara too, after just one dance. How pathetic is that? If Sara Rothman was at the other end of something real for me, maybe I could do anything too. Like on the bus, I wouldn't care if it hurt me – my brain would just shut off because love gives you this *power*. But, I guess love gives you the power to just say *adios* to your family too if they move across the country.

"And Bucky says it's okay?" I ask my sister. "You know, to live with him?"

"He loves me, Larry, I thought I just told you that. When you love somebody, it doesn't matter how old you are, or, or, where you live, just as long as you can be together as much as possible. I mean, can't you see that?"

"Sure," I say, trying to just agree. We both stare at his stupid 2B door.

"He's not home now, of course. He's at work. My man works, you know."

"Sure," I say again. What am I supposed to say? I don't want to say anything really, because I can't stop imagining going across the country in a big ol' truck with all of our stuff.. .*without* Marna. Just me and my parents. How broken is that?

"I'd miss you," I say out loud, soft, and more pathetic than I really want.

"Yeah," she says, biting her bottom lip. "There's that."

"I will." Damn.

"Okay, but. . .now you know where I'll be if you need me," she says, patting my head like I'm a puppy or something. "Apartment 2B."

I don't want to talk anymore because I don't want to think about it. "Can we go back?" I say.

We are headed back from apartment 2B, apparently my sister's future home and I'm out in front this time, full of a new energy – an empty, depressed and angry energy. I just want to pedal and breathe and hear myself do the work. I've got my head down and I chug up the big hill of Kressen Road when all of a sudden I see this other biker coming right at me on my side of the road. It's like I look up, see him, and then our bikes crash into each other. That's how fast it happens.

The kid, a couple years younger than me at least, maybe ten years old (and even a few inches shorter), gets up and wipes the street off his hands just like I do. We're okay, I mean there were no cars coming or anything, no blood either, but it's got my heart racing a million miles a second. Marna slams her brakes behind me and jumps off her bike.

My sister starts freaking out on this random kid. "What are you doing?!"

"I'm, I'm sorry," says the kid. He's trying to mount his bike again, escape, but Marna is right there, going after him with her pointer finger.

"You know, you were riding on the wrong side of the road!" She's yelling. Not as loud as my mom, but if you closed your eyes. . .

"I'm sorry," this kid says. He can't seem to get out of her way so he can get back on his bike and leave this scene intact.

"Marna, stop," I try to say louder than her, but that's impossible.

"No! This kid needs to learn the bicycle rules! Do you know the bicycle rules?!" She's asking like my mom does when she's lost it; now Marna's the one berating this boy with questions she really doesn't want him to answer. "The bicycle rules state that you always, always, ALWAYS ride on the right side of the road! Do you know the difference between your right and left?! Do you?!"

The kid is quivering, wanting to reach for his other handle bar, but he's afraid Marna's going to lunge and eat him whole. She's taller than him. Bigger. And he's stuck.

"Marna, quit!" I say louder. My insides start to rattle, a familiar hum.

"What if a car ran over my brother's arm or leg?! Or worse?! Huh?!" She's literally two inches from the kid's face, hovering, screaming into his forehead.

"Marna, leave him alone!" I put my kickstand down and jump in front of her, sort of boxing her out. "He gets it!"

I back up toward the curb, making Marna back up too, giving the kid enough room to escape. He hops on his bike like he's a cowboy suddenly being chased by Indians and peddles across Kressen Road to the *right* side. Marna darts out into the middle of the street, yelling, "That's it! Run away you wormy little coward!!"

"Hey?!" I yell, as a car zooms by in front of me.

"What?!" Marna says, whipping around, now completely in the turn lane.

She's still glaring in his direction before snapping out of her raging hypnotic state, finally realizing she's in the middle of Kressen Road. She coolly returns to her bike. As she swings her leg over her seat and snaps on her helmet, she says, "Well, are you okay?"

Marna is barely breathing hard. It's like she became the Incredible Hulk, and now she's switched back to Bruce Banner. I can't stop staring at her. She just might be a dragon. Or. . .my mom. Or my dad when he loses his temper. I don't know.

"Let's just go home," I finally say. "You lead."

"Fine. Let's just go home," she says. Then she smiles, a maniacal smile, kicks up her kickstand and peddles fast.

I can hardly keep up.

CHAPTER THIRTY-SEVEN

This will be my fifth visit to Dr. Stone and I can't wait to tell him about testing for my green belt. That's right, I'm officially green; passing all testing requirements with "exceeds expectations," including three rounds of sparring. I've discovered that it helps to be small for sparring, because it doesn't give your opponent a whole lot to try and hit. I'm starting to wonder whether I may be a pretty good fighter.

I've already told Dr. Stone about Sara Rothman – that happened during visits 2, 3 and 4 – and her mysterious letter capturing her mysterious life in Israel. Actually, I showed the letter to Dr. Stone because I had it with me. If I'm being honest, I keep her letter with me all of the time. As far as the mystery in Sara's letter where she says, ". . . it was soooooo good to hear from you. . ." (with 7 Os in her "so"), Dr. Stone keeps "wondering" if my sister swiped one of my letters from this summer and sent it to Sara, even though I told him Marna swore up and down that she didn't. And even though I counted and all the letters were still there.

"This is the same sib that stole Girl Scout cookies," he says, with a grin.

But I don't tell Dr. Stone about the actual letter I did write back to Sara because I don't want to talk about why I haven't mailed it, and I know he'd ask.

I don't want to talk about Robert Bullock either, and how it's not stopping on the bus, how it's worse, how flicks on the ear have become punches on my arms or backhand slaps to my chest, and how more kids on the bus gather around my seat when Robert does what he does, no matter where I choose to sit. Because I'm not on the bus right now, I'd like to not think about the bus. Even though I'm in a shrink's office and supposed to.

And I'm not going to tell him about running into Kevin today right before I took the bus home, him trying to act like nothing ever happened. He was all, "Hey, Ratner, where you been?" He never used to call me "Ratner," but now everyone calls me Ratner. "I've been where I've been," I said to Kevin. "The old neighborhood."

"Alright then," he started to leave. He looked over my head and smiled 'cause he saw his friends. "I gotta jet, but hey, do you still go up on the roof?"

"No," I lied.

"Man, we gotta get back up there. We do." Then he just ran off.

All that, I'm not telling Dr. Stone.

We're in the parking lot. Today we are playing good ol' fashioned catch with a baseball and gloves. This guy has a lot of equipment. I'm not big into baseball anymore, but I love the sound the ball makes when it hits the pocket of a glove perfectly.

He's asking me how I feel when my dad goes on and on about his glory sports days because apparently I've men- tioned it a lot in sessions. I tell him, yes, sort of, that I wish I could be as good at sports like my dad was, or funny like my dad is, or that I could hit Robert Bullock first and keep hitting him until somebody pulls me off. . .like my dad. But mostly, I wish my dad would tell my mom to calm down. I mean, I know the strike and stuff, but still.

Dr. Stone nods, the kind of nod he does when he wants to fully digest what I've said. "That's a tough dynamic, Larry."

He takes a huge breath and lets it out, then looks at his watch. "We should head back to the office." He throws the ball to me and I catch it, take off the glove and wait for him to button up his shirt.

At the office, Dr. Stone looks at his watch again. That's twice with the watch. Weird. He seems nervous today, and he never seems nervous. I sit in my usual chair, and Dr. Stone rolls his out from behind the desk and sits right across from me.

"Look, we were originally approved for five visits," he says. "This is the fifth."

"Wait," I say, realizing. "This is our last appointment? What do you mean?"

He nods. "Look, it could be about money too, with the strike. That's fair to throw in the mix, you know?" He hesitates and then says, "But it's okay. . .okay?"

"Whatever," I say, with a ton of Marna-like attitude.

"It's not 'whatever,' no way." For the first time, Dr. Stone seems kind of agitated, but he doesn't yell or throw tissue boxes at me; he just takes a giant breath and then looks at me in my eyes like he does. All strong, making me look back. "I want to be sure that you know you've made significant progress here."

"Yeah, but now we're done," I say, way more pouty than I want to be.

"True," he says, walking over after dropping off the baseball gloves in the closet. He sits on the edge of his desk instead of the big foamy shrink chair. "So now you have to find alternatives, other people that you can trust and communicate with."

"Who?"

"What about your parents?"

"I can't talk to them." Right. I should go talk to my parents and tell them to let me continue coming to Dr. Stone so that I don't have to talk to my parents.

"They brought you here in the first place," he says, scooting all the way to the front of his chair, looking all intense in my eyes. "That has to count for something."

"My own blood, right?" I say with an attitude. What a bunch of crap.

Dr. Stone probably doesn't hear *my own blood* crap a lot, how I hear it constantly, like a big soapy bubble that pops before your finger can touch it. Like a lousy piece of shrink advice.

"Fine," I say, still way more pouty than I want to sound.

"And, well, maybe a friend," he says, emphasizing the last word.

"I told you, I don't have any friends." I look down, away from Dr. Stone's eyes, and try to suck it up, keep it in, keep it together. Damn.

"Larry," he says, leaning forward. "I have two true friends in my life. My wife. She's my best friend. And my mom, even though she's a pain in my butt. Sure, I *hang* with people, but a true friend loves you unconditionally, no matter how *tall* you are. Those people who you think have lots of friends don't have real friends. They're just as lonely as you. Look, don't force it, but be open. It might be right under your nose. . ."

"Who?"

"I don't know," he says. But, c'mon, clearly he knows. Dr. Stone knows all.

"Sara?" Her name just comes out of me. He doesn't answer, just grins. Irritating. "But she's on the other side of the planet. I can't even—" I stop myself, realizing I'm just whining, and look up at Dr. Stone's eyes. He locks onto mine, the way he can do sometimes, his eyes almost talking, saying, *uh-uh-uh, look at me, stay right here. . .*

"It's been great to meet you, Larry. You're a special kid." And then Dr. Stone gives me a hug. The first doctor to do that. I feel like crying, like I'm saying goodbye to another friend moving out of the old neighborhood that I'll never see again. Or out of the country, halfway across the world, where they shoot rockets and your family has a bomb shelter next to the mailbox.

Tattoo Show-N-Tell #6. . . February Installment

*O*n my back, here, is a fire-spittin' dragon. 'Cause I love drag-ons. Some are nice fantastic monsters. They give little boys and girls like ya a ride, fly ya around the world on their backs. But one day, and ya never know when it's comin', a dragon is gonna spit out all the fire that's been cookin' inside of 'em. Eh? And that doesn't make 'em bad monsters, eh? It makes 'em perfect dragons.

Okay then, sit back, sit down, and sit up straight. Here we go. Oh, and don't piss on my bus.

CHAPTER THIRTY-EIGHT

The Philadelphia School District teachers' strike is getting to my parents more and more every day. Especially my mom. Yesterday, we all gathered around the TV and watched the news announcing the whole school year is officially cancelled. My mom actually started crying as soon as the superintendent started speaking. It was sad to see; I thought maybe I should hug her, but then I didn't move to do it.

I did English Town with my dad today, but we only sold two comforters. And again, it was a cold silent outing. When we get home, my mom is still in her terrycloth bathrobe and her hair is all crazy from sleeping, or maybe not sleeping enough. She is rummaging through the freezer, taking all the stuff out of it, looking for something. With her crazy hair head still in the freezer, she asks my dad how much we sold today.

"Not enough," he says, tossing his car keys on the counter.

"It was cold," I say. It's not officially winter yet, but it was freezing out.

Actually, I'm in a relatively good mood for a guy that spent several hours freezing his butt off in a flea market. Even though my dad hardly talked to me, he did let me check Facebook on his phone while we were waiting for pretty much nobody to buy comforters. I immediately went to Sara Rothman's page and saw she posted this: *Went to work with Dad today. Played catch with my friends from the other side of the wall. One day, soon, I'm going to figure out a way, a path, something, where I can go over there and meet my friends. While it doesn't matter to me what they look like, I'd really like to see them! Peace out.*

It just made me feel good. She went to work with her dad and I was at work with my dad, so it's like we were together at work with our dads, a million miles away. . . And while I didn't leave a comment, I did "like" it, which is the extent of what I do on Facebook.

My dad gently pulls my mom out of our freezer and kisses her on her lips. They have a regular greeting ritual – two quick kisses on the lips no matter what. "Two comforters?" she asks. "That's it?"

"It was cold, that's why," I say. "It wasn't Dad's fault."

"If it's cold, people need comforters," she says. "They need comfort. Do you think you stayed long enough?"

"People were lookin' but not buyin', Dear," he says, somewhat defeated, somewhat irritated. "And then people stopped lookin'. So we came home."

By now my mom has piled the rest of the freezer contents onto the counter. Whatever she's looking for, she can't seem to find. I have this familiar feeling, like I'd rather be anywhere but here in the kitchen. It's sort of how people feel right before a storm with a tornado in its path, but in my house, as soon as you think a storm's coming, there is no path, the tornado is right on you.

"Marna!" My mom yells. "Get down here!" See, anyone can put some volume into their voice so it makes it out of the kitchen and up the stairs, but when my mom's in this state, her voice seeps through all the walls too.

"Dan, you didn't eat the Salisbury steak TV dinner, did you?" she asks.

"Nope," he says.

"Did you, Larry?" she asks me.

"Double nope." Like I said, I'm still in a good mood.

"Well, I don't understand how food is disappearing around here but nobody seems to be eating it—Marna, get down here right now!"

And it's on. Seriously. I've seen this scene before. Marna comes down, says, "What? Like, I was on the phone."

"When I call you, sister, you better damn well get off the phone and get down here. You understand me?"

During these times nobody is sure if you're actually supposed to answer questions or just let them ring in the air. Marna sighs but says nothing.

"Did you eat the Salisbury steak TV dinner?" my mom asks, holding court.

"No way," Marna snaps back. "I don't even like steak. And I don't eat meat; I've announced this to everybody. Several times. Now can I go back—?"

"Nobody is going anywhere until we find out who ate the Salisbury steak TV dinner that I *just* bought two days ago and now has mysteriously disappeared."

Unfortunately, I am right. I have seen this scene before. We all will stay here and tell the truth as we see it, and we will go nowhere.

"I guess we must have gremlins living here," my mom says to my dad.

"I guess," my dad adds, mostly because he doesn't know what else to say. He knows my mom expects him to say something, to participate in this slow torture, but he hasn't read the handbook or something. Actually, I believe he wants to go, be done, and get on with life, but he's stuck too. Almost like on the bus, my mom follows me, no matter which seat I choose, and sits right next to me. We're all stuck.

"Larry, why don't you just 'fess up so we can get the heck out of this kitchen?" Marna says, elbowing me in the ribs.

"I didn't eat it so there's nothing to 'fess up about," I say.

"You did too," she says. Now, Marna and I are fighting like two five-year-olds. Did not. Did too. Did not. Did too. And blah, blah, blah.

"I didn't," I say. "And how do you know what I ate or didn't eat?"

"You're the only one—process of elimination."

My mom is staring at my dad while my sister and I go back and forth. Waiting for him to fix it, she says, "You're just going to sit there and say nothing?"

"What do you want me to say?" he asks, hands locked behind his head.

I'm wondering what in fact she does want him to say or do.

"This is great," she starts. My mom is at the bottom and she's going up, up, up. "Say nothing, Dan. What I'll do is continue to buy things, with the money we *don't* have, and then we'll all watch them disappear, and you can just say nothing. That's how we'll spend our unemployment time and our limitless amount of income that will be pouring in from our now monumental comforter sales!"

"They're liars," my dad says, like it's all useless. "What are you gonna do?"

"I guess what we always do, Dan, let me handle every-thing: the organizing, the disciplining of the children, everything, while you give me absolutely no support!"

Marna jabs me in my ribs again, harder. "'Fess up, you idiot."

"I didn't eat it," I say. Because I didn't. In the midst of all this, I'm wondering what the big deal is about the dang TV dinner and who would lie about eating it.

"Clearly, they think money grows on trees," is the best my dad can come up with.

To which my mom replies, "You kids think money grows on trees?"

"No," we both say.

"Apparently when we sat the kids down and told them that we're on strike, that there's no money coming in and not to be wasteful, they didn't understand," my dad says. In these times, when my mom wants him to do something about something that he doesn't know what to do, he talks about us like we're not in the room.

"We told you. . ." my mom says, but doesn't finish. She is in that weird and wild place of almost crying, but then that goes away, and just becomes, I don't even know. Something else though, that I don't think I'll ever understand.

"Well, no one is leaving this kitchen until someone decides to tell the truth," my mom says with her crazy hair and ratty bathrobe (I hate all bathrobes in the whole world!). Her eyes are now popping out of her head. It's on.

"Fine. I ate it," Marna says because she knows it's on too. "Even though I didn't. There. I ate it. How much do I owe you? I'm sorry you wanted the Salisbury steak TV dinner and I ate it even though I didn't."

My mom looks at my dad. My dad looks at me.

"What?" I say. "I didn't eat it either. Maybe you miscounted."

My dad lights up because he finally thinks of something to contribute: "Your mother did not miscount. She's not a, a miscounter, first off, and second off, with the strike here, we're counting *everything*. We've told you this."

"You're a liar," my mother yells at me. "Both of you. This is a joke. I'm trying to get the truth out of two juveniles who steal Girl Scout cookies." Then she points at me and spits, "I did not miscount."

I want to put exclamation points at the end of each of my mom's sentences, but I'm afraid they might not properly represent the volume levels. Everything is screaming. And she's got spit collected at the corners of her mouth. There is a ringing in my ears; the word "liar" is like a symbol inside my eardrum and I wish I could lie about whether I'm lying or not, but I'm just not smart enough. The truth is I don't know what the right thing to do is, or frankly, what the big deal is.

"Answer me!" my mom yells, and it startles me, sending a jolt through my body. It shouldn't be shocking me, but clearly there are parts of my body that still don't know how this all goes.

"I didn't eat the dinner, I didn't do it," I say.

"You're a liar!" my mom barks back.

"I'm not." I think I'm crying now. No, I'm not. I'm, I'm just shaking a little.

"You are a liar!" She points at me. "No one could have done it but you, and you are just going to stand there and lie to my face!"

"I'm not lying." Now I think I'm on the edge of crying, even though I don't want to. Because I don't cry.

"You are and you know it. And I'll tell you something else, Buster, we're not leaving this kitchen until—Dan are you just going to stand there and let him get me upset like this?! With my blood pressure through the roof! Are you going to participate in the discipline of this child?!"

My dad grabs the garbage can and violently pulls the garbage bag out, causing me and Marna to flinch. Then he turns the entire bag upside down, spilling the trash all over the counter next to the pile of the now-defrosting freezer items that my mom took out when this all started. My dad is smacking the trash around the counter, looking for the TV dinner box like a starving alley cat.

"Dan, what are you doing?" my mom yells.

"Finding the box." He slams down more trash.

"You're being ridiculous!" my mom yells.

"I'm doing *something!*" my dad yells. "And then we'll make the perpetrator eat the box too! Huh? How's about that?!" My dad is totally out of control and not one bit funny. Garbage is flying everywhere.

Marna is whimpering now as well. We start screaming, louder and louder at each other, on top of each other. She screams, "Oh just stop, okay, admit it—"

"I swear I didn't eat it—" I say.

"He's lying—" Marna says.

"I'm not a liar—"

"Stop it, stop it, stop—" Marna just keeps yelling "stop it" over me.

My mom screams louder than all of us, louder than this house can really hold, "We're not going anywhere until somebody tells the truth!"

Suddenly, there is a loud BANG as the trash can flies across the room and slams into the kitchen wall.

And then my dad is on me like the fastest thing that's ever happened.

This is not a spanking or a "licking," as my dad has called it. Getting spanked has a sting to it, sure, from a belt or a hand to the skin on the butt. Or skin on underwear. A spanking has a rhythm to it as well. The spanker counts the whacks, maybe under his breath or in his head. But, here, now, there's no belt and no open hand; and no counting or space between whacks. People say that the waiting is the worst part of it, right? Like when we stole the Girl Scout cookies. The anticipation beats up your brain for hours and then the spanker (my dad) comes home and finishes the deal by smacking your (my) butt.

BUT. . .I don't think the waiting is the worst part at all, because when you're waiting for a spanking, at least you know it's coming.

NOW, though, there is a bigger man attacking me and I didn't know it was coming.

This whole year my dad keeps telling me that I should hit Robert Bullock *first* and don't stop until someone pulls me off. That's how you do it, he has told me. He was trying to teach me. And now, I'm really learning it.

I don't tell people that my dad has a TEMPER. Not Dr. Stone. Not in a letter to Sara Rothman. Only Snowball. Of course, my sister knows too. One time, when Marna was in the same sort of position I'm in now, I saw my dad snap and drag her up the stairs by her hair. You could hear the bump of the stairs as her butt hit them on the way up, and then there were a few no butt-to-stair non-beats because he actually lifted her high enough to miss the last four stairs.

That's a TEMPER. And now it's on me.

People always say a person "loses" his temper. But I think, like with my dad here, he doesn't lose it, he actually FINDS it, and his TEMPER is now smothering and punching.. .*finding* me. I don't want to make excuses for him, but it is almost like his TEMPER becomes an entity in and of itself – a *bully* that takes over my dad's body.

There's no smack sounds when your father is beating you up. It's all *hard.* Everything that hits you is hard. You hear your own breathing and your own screaming, like it's coming from somebody else's body at somebody else's house. I'm thinking that maybe this is it, the end. I don't mean to come off all Hollywood, but that's what I'm thinking. Like the prisoners in the concentration camps who would just throw themselves on the electric fences that held them captive inside the camps. I can understand why those people would choose to end it all. At least then it's on your own terms, like whatever was on the other side of this beating has got to be better than a life of being beaten.

It keeps coming. Hard. No real noise. Just breathing. Cement knuckles. . .

And then, my mom, somehow, pulls my father off of me with her body and her voice. *This* is how real fights end.

It's weird. For a time, while my dad was on me, I couldn't hear my mom screaming, "You're a liar," and all that stupid TV dinner stuff. I didn't really even hear her stop him, and I wonder if the TEMPER that became my dad maybe wanted to stop hearing it too. Maybe he was going out of his mind and needed a way out. Like I was the electric fence that *he* jumped on so the life he was living at that moment would end.

"Look," Marna says amongst all the breathing in the room. She points at me, "His eye." I'm not really feeling any pain, but I'm crying 'cause. . .I don't even know why. I touch below my eye. It's puffy and big. My dad turns away and goes to the window to look outside like he's waiting for the police to come and cuff him.

My mom bends down to take a closer look. Out of habit she asks my dad's opinion. "Dan, look at his eye," like I'm trying on a pair of shoes. "Is he okay?"

My dad walks back to me, reaches for my face. I wince and pull away hard. Maybe my body is thinking my dad is going to pound on me again. All I know is I don't want my father – whose job it is to feel where our big toes come to, who made me make 100 left-handed layups one day, who is always silly – to get near me anymore, let alone touch my swollen face.

He sees me flinch and goes back to the window, nods his head.

Somehow, I'm on the floor in my mom's arms, rocking gently. I can feel her heart beating hard and fast in my ear.

"See?" she says in this shaky voice. "You're lucky I was here to pull your father off of you. It should never get to the point where he gets that angry. Which doesn't excuse him. . .that's not what I'm saying." My sister returns from the kitchen and gives my mom something. My mom says, "Here, put this over your eye." It's the ice pack that I used to use when I got migraines in the middle of the night. My mom would hold me like she is now and place the pack on my forehead and say, "It's okay" over and over.

"I hate this place," Marna says loud enough for everyone to hear it, but soft enough for everyone to know she was only talking to herself.

What should I do now?

Marna would go pack her bags. Someday, she's going to open her bedroom door and leave with all her bags and her books and everything, go into some car, and I'll never see her again; her cell phone lonely and broken in the middle of her stripped bed. I swear, if she ever leaves, I don't know what I'll do. And that's the truth.

My mom softly asks me, "Are you okay?" and it's like asking the question out loud also makes her cry. I can't help it.

I bawl like a little baby, and I'm heaving a little bit, trying to breathe, trying to speak, I think. I want to say something but I can't even catch my breath. How pathetic am I? If the rabbi and the cantor saw me like this, they'd snatch my bar mitzvah certificate away.

CHAPTER THIRTY-NINE

It's not morning yet, but I feel something moving in my room. I'm so passed out that even though my brain is saying there's somebody or something in my room – danger! danger! – my body won't let me even open my eyes. The beat in my head is exactly that, a throbbing, jackhammering headache cooking in my brain. My eyes take 10 seconds to finally flutter open, because if I go faster my skull will shatter like a light bulb.

All I can really see is a giant headgear right under my nose. It hurts to make my eyeballs look down my face, past my nostrils, but there's no way I'm moving my head. It's crazy-glued to my pillow.

"Do you have any money?" the headgear asks.

"What? No—"

"They have to fall asleep at some point and when they do, we can go, get, scat, scoot, get the heck outta dodge." I think it's my sister.

"Marna?"

"I would do it for you," she's talking super fast and choppy. "Even though you didn't do it for me. . .you know, when Dad did what he did to you to me. Remember? At the old house? 'Cause she got him all worked up? Only he never full-out punched me in the face. And you're younger and didn't have access to a car, so I forgive you." She takes a giant breath. "I could call Bucky and he could meet us at the 7-Eleven and take us to the bus station. We could cut and dye our hair and change our names and be orphans—"

"Bus station—"

"Do you want some Pixy Stix?"

Just the sound of pixy and stix hurts and makes me close my eyes.

"I've been eating them all night," she says.

"Huh?"

"Like coffee, while waiting for the guards to go down. I bought a whole box - sixty-four Pixy Stix. I don't like grape. You could have the grape ones."

"No."

"Shhh." Marna leans over and almost touches my eye. "OMG, Larry," she says. "It looks like someone stuffed a globe in your eye socket. Are you okay?"

I try to nod that I'm okay, but I can't move my head. Marna takes two steps away from my bed and two steps towards my bed, over and over. She's pacing I guess. I don't know for sure because I can't really focus. "I don't have much money anymore because I recently made a rather bold purchase on some accessories, but had I known that the world was going to flip upside-down in our own house, I would have saved, saved, saved." She is talking so fast and so weird, I'm not sure what I've got here – a sister or a pixy.

"Marna, is that – what time is it?"

"It's dealin' time, it's time to put up or shut down. Time to show the bosses who's boss. Time to knick and to knack and to paddy-whack and get your bones out of bed. We're takin' the midnight train to Georgia. . .or Philadelphia, whichever one is closer."

"What? Why? And I'm not going anywhere 'til my head stops dinging."

"Oh," she says, then quickly sashays over to my bed and sits at the foot of it. She tries to ask softly, "But you're okay? Okay? 'Cause let me just say this one thing. . .If he hurt you, you know – permanent? Like if you can't see the way you used to see? Or anything. We can sue our own parents. I Googled child abuse laws in New Jersey. Statute 9.6.1 section B states, and I quote,'. . .inflicting upon a child unnecessary suffering or pain, either mental or physical. . .' I've seen it on the news too. But it's best for the case if there's permanent damage."

Marna actually finishes her sentence and takes a full breath for the first time since she's been in my room. She inhales two more Pixy Stix.

"Besides," I say, almost dreaming. "If I went anywhere, I'd go to Israel."

"Wait, what?!" Marna squeals, but smacks both hands over her own mouth, stifling her excitement so as to not alert the guards. And then she makes one of those gushing girl sounds. "For her, right? For that Sara chick."

I close my eyes and she grabs my chin and yanks my face towards her. My headache screams but I open my eyes. Marna, now two inches from my face, all retainer headgear, says, "You *dog*. My brother, the dog. A young pup, totally in love."

I swipe her hand off of my face and we sit here in the dark and the silence, my eyes heavier than I can manage, just waiting. For what I don't really know.

"Is Dad—is he. . .?" I finally ask, eyes still closed.

"Downstairs. He never went to sleep. They both didn't, haven't. She keeps talkin' about the budget and what other part-time job he could get, and what other things they could sell besides comforters. . . and he just keeps staring out the window."

"Oh," I say.

"But they check on you. Constantly."

"He was in here?" I ask, the thought of it making my eye ache too.

"Mostly her. But it's on the hour, every hour. So if you want to make a run for it, we have to do it soon 'cause she just checked on you. We only have a window of time. A window. They keep bringing you water. You've got eight glasses over there. Thirsty?"

My mouth is kind of dry, but to raise my head and body to be in some kind of position to drink feels impossible and stupid. The thought of it makes me sleepy and I think my eyelids are falling anyway.

"Okay, okay, okay," Marna says, nudging, waking me up. I'm not sure if I was asleep for a second or a whole day. "When you feel better, you just say the word and we're outta here. You just say the word."

"Thanks," I think I say.

"Good. No, thank you. Good. Well, I'm either gonna go to sleep or take a shower. One of the two and not in that order. Good night, little brother."

I think the words "good night" in my head, but I have a feeling I never said them. My eyes are too heavy and I feel them closing slow and hard, like a giant draw bridge. Before my eyes fully close, I see the skinny shadow of my sister sneakily slink over to my dresser, where there are several cups of water waiting for me. I think for a brief moment that she's thirsty, that maybe I'm dreaming about my sister snatching several sips of water from my dresser, but I must be immediately dreaming because each sip sounds like the crinkling of paper, the shuffling of envelopes. . .and then I'm totally out.

CHAPTER FORTY

In the morning, I wake up with a killer headache. It's lighter outside and even though it's still dark in my room, I'm sensing something is wrong. I turn and see that I forgot to set my alarm clock. "Jeez," I say and try to pop out of bed, but when the pain in my head thumps harder, I drop back to my pillow and wait for the percussion to settle back down to a manageable throbbing level.

"We wanted to let you sleep," my dad says. He's sitting in my Philadelphia Eagles chair, and for God knows how long. "I did your route. Don't worry."

"What about school?" I somehow mutter, trying not to grimace in pain.

"Maybe you take the day off today," he says all gentle.

"But I don't think I have a fever." That's always been the rule in our house: Unless you have a fever, you go to school. Your leg could be hanging from your body, attached only by a nerve ending, but no fever = you go to school.

"Sometimes it's good to just take the day off," my dad says.

There's a silence that's not so familiar to me with my dad in the room. Usually he's goofing around. And during baseball season, the first thing I'd always ask him is who won the Phillies game last night. But there was never this, this silence.

"I brought you an ice pack for your eye. . .and some Tylenol if your head hurts. Does your head hurt?"

I think about that question and swallow, "No."

"Well, it's here if you need it." He comes over to me with the ice pack. I don't flinch. My dad looks really tired and he stares at my eye. It's sort of freaky how he's being. "Here, wrap this towel around it. Good. Helps with the swelling."

I do it. This is my first black eye and if I'm telling the truth, I can't wait to see what it looks like in the mirror. But right now the thumping in my head has settled to a low simmer, but I know if I get up, it will boil up to a pounding percussion. Plus, my dad is sitting on my bed, looking at me. He never does this.

My dad takes a deep breath and says, "See I, well, I have a temper." Usually he's so smooth when he talks, stories roll off his tongue, but now he struggles, little grunts of awkward utterances. "No. No. That's not—" It suddenly comes back to me that Marna was in here last night trying to get me to run away. "I think what happens is I can't make any of it *right*, you know, and, and it gets all in me or all over me and I can't control that. Wait, that's not—I have trouble controlling—I mean, I *need* to control that. I need to get that done."

"It's okay—" I finally say, even though it isn't.

"But, see, you, you're not like that," he says, all excited suddenly.

"I have a temper too," I say, almost sitting up, flexing, my head thumping.

"Okay," he says. "Sure. But, but not like me. I didn't *give* that to you."

I know my dad is trying to say this nice thing, but it's really bothering me. Of all the things not to give me, why not give me his temper? I could really use it.

"I didn't eat the stupid TV dinner," I say with more anger than I really want.

My head pounds saying that, but for some reason, it makes me sound threatening, and I feel almost tough, and it's worth the pain if that makes sense.

"It doesn't matter," he says.

It does matter to me because when it happened I didn't understand why it mattered. But then I don't understand why my mom gets aggravated over almost everything anyway. I mean, I know the strike and all, but still.

"Larry, I'm sorry I hit you," my dad says, trying to look me in my eyes, the way he taught me to do. But it's probably just like staring at the scene of the crime – my right eye, swollen and blue. He swallows, makes himself look again.

I know my dad is trying to apologize, but it's just making me angry. My throat gets tight and I take a big breath, close my eyes so my head stops pounding and finally say, "It doesn't really hurt."

"C'mon, get dressed," my dad says as he pulls my shades up to let the day in. "We can go get a hoagie or something else low key."

"Dad?" I say, and he stops at my door.

Usually this would be when I ask him who won the Phillies game last night, and he'd tell me on his way out of my room. It's all weird now, but he's waiting, stuck, not leaving my room at all. Instead, I clear my throat and finally say, "I want to go to school." My dad looks stumped. Before he can say anything, I say, "Take me." Not in a bossy way, but I can see how it might come off that way, so I say, "Please?"

My dad sighs. Nods. His face looks like I punched him in the stomach.

CHAPTER FORTY-ONE

L ast period of the day is PE, but one of my parents must
have called the school to tell them I can't do PE today
because Coach Stack sends me back to English class where
Mrs. Grammar Tree sends me to the computer lab to work
on my compare and contrast essay. Both of them are all ten-
tative when they're talking to me, squinting at my swollen
black eye I'm sure.

So far, amazingly, no one has asked me how my bloated
face got this way. Maybe it's not so amazing. I haven't really
been engaging in conversations of any kind at school lately,
so not much has changed. That's just true.

My headache is really thumping right now, and I haven't
felt like eating all day. Actually, maybe people were avoiding
me today because I pretty much look like a zombie with a
dotted eye. Scary. I kind of like the thought of that though.

The computer lab is a room in the back of the library,
and right now I'm the only person in it. The librarian set me
up on a computer and is now out in the main room leading
a 6th grade class through a research project.

So I get on Facebook, Sara Rothman's page. Oh my
God, I can't believe it. . .today's status says:

Dad just told me his work here wraps up this month and that
we are moving back "home" next month. Wow. I thought I was
going to be here forever. I thought I was gonna learn how to shoot

a gun when I was 18, you know, join the Israeli army? Guess not. Tomorrow I go to my dad's job for the last time. I swear, tomorrow's the day I meet my friends for the first time! Face to face. Yup. Excited all the way around! USA – We'll be home soon!

It hurts my eye to smile, seriously, but I can't help it. If Snowball were here, I'd read Sara's post out loud to him, and we'd both bark for joy.

"What happened to your eye, son?" I hear the librarian ask me from the front of the computer lab, and I quickly click out of Facebook because we're not allowed on the Internet without permission. I'm supposed to be comparing and contrasting, not status checking.

"I. . ." Just as I'm about to answer with some lie I haven't thought of yet, the bell rings and I say, ". . .gotta catch my bus." And I push the computer button to shut down and scurry past the librarian, my head pounding all kinds of percussion-related havoc as I race to the bus.

Bring on the pain though. Because Sara Rothman is coming home. It hurts my face to smile, but I can't help it.

CHAPTER FORTY-TWO

There's a substitute bus driver today. She's a black lady with grey hair and a big jangling keychain with laminated pictures on the ring, probably photos of all her grandchildren. I *was* in a good mood.

Robert Bullock picked me. He is at least two feet taller than me today. I can hear him growing as he comes up the bus steps; step by step, getting TALLER, like a ticking thing getting closer and closer. Or maybe that's just my pounding headache.

And if I were his size, or even three inches taller than I am, no way does he pick me. Today I am in the back, one seat from the back window, because it doesn't matter where I sit. He'll find me. If I sit on the driver's lap, he'll find me.

As soon as he walks on the bus, chanting my last name, swinging his backpack in his right hand, I try not to look at him because today I just don't feel good: my head, my eye, everything. I wish there was a hiding place in between the seats or a time-out section of the bus, or that I was just home.

But I wanted to be tough, like my dad, and gut out the school day. I didn't want him sitting home, babysitting me, or at some hoagie place feeling all sorry for me. No way. I'm a man now.

I don't think about Sara Rothman anymore, can't even remember what she looks like. My headache has mutated, also pounding in my swollen eye, and as I watch Robert come up the bus stairs, I can't help thinking about my dad's lost and found temper.

I've tried each section on the bus; this is a promise I've made to my mother who is ready to call the principal again and the bus driver again. There is room today for Robert Bullock in the last seat where he belongs, last, but he'll have to pass me to get there. Today he is all happy, and as usual, chants my last name before he even walks up the bus steps. I'm looking out the window, hoping to ignore and be ignored.

But as he strolls past me, he swings his book bag high above his head, like he's about to stick the magic sword into the boulder. From way above *his* head, he drops the bag on *my* head; it lands and sort of melts down my skull.

My body can't even compute what just happened.

He takes his backpack off of my head, like he's scooping up a ground ball on one hop, and simply takes his seat behind me. I hear my name over and over and "Where'd you get that dotted eye, Ratner?" Over and over . . .

My body starts to register the pain, and I am surprised by it. The pain.

I know my eyes are full of tears like when you get hit in the nose, but at school, they will call it crying and add that to my list. The list grows, but I don't. When I was younger, my parents taught me not to fight, to talk it out and solve my problems with words. But I know they have lost their patience too. They want me to kick Robert Bullock's butt. That's as true as the smoke on my dad's breath.

My eye is pulsing, my neck stinging, and my head is killing me. . .again.

Robert Bullock is two feet taller than me and I can't remember that anymore because I am hitting him in the face NOW. I am turned around, my eyes still leaking, and I am punching him and he isn't smiling.

Usually in a fight, someone has to pull the fighters apart. That's what my dad always taught me. It's what he showed me last night when my mom had to "save me."

Is this a fight? Robert Bullock is not hitting back and no one is pulling me off of him. Robert's arms go up and down, but they are like twigs. Everything that I learned in karate is out the bus window: how to punch, how to kick, how to manage my anger. I'm using none of it. My arms and fists fly around like giant, wild windmill wings coming from any and every direction. As far as fighting goes, it's 100% ugly.

When I hit a piece of his arm, it snaps back and smacks his face. You would think that his arms would cover his face, but I can still see his eyes and his teeth. His teeth. Big and white. They must be magnets because my right fist and then my left connect with Bullock's teeth. There's no *thwap* sound like before. Plus it's a hard thing against my knuckles – only hard, not soft – like I'm punching a collection of bones. I should hurt, I think it hurts, but I don't feel it. Not a thing. No stinging. No head aching. No nothing.

I'm waiting for somebody or some bodies to pull me off of Robert Bullock. While I wait, my arms keep flailing at him, on him. There is no real sound I can hear, just breathing, even though I really want to hear all of the commentary because, supposedly, the whole year has been about this moment. But I can't hear anything except my own runaway breathing, and somehow, some semblance of cheering. It makes me go faster. Faster. On and on I go. But there is no blood—

Red splinters onto his shirt.

Blood.

I see that. Blood. On his shirt. Now in his mouth. His teeth are red and white. They look like tiny candy canes. My body sees it and my body loves it. More, more, more. Some of his, some of mine from my knuckles? My body loves it. Some of it drips like tears and then smears onto his chin.

Shouldn't somebody pull me off?

My body keeps going, flailing away, telling my brain to shut the heck up. My body is smiling at the blood. Laughing for the blood.

My brain wants to figure this out. My brain wants to talk to my body and negotiate with what it has now found: My lost TEMPER. My body introduces my lost temper to Robert Bullock's face.

A clean shot. His nose fits in between my top two knuckles and my body knows how perfect a punch that is. And not because of karate. There's no karate in anything that's going on here. 'Cause in karate I have to think about how to do it. No. I'm just punching. Again. And again. His arms are heavy twigs. A clean shot. His head smacks the back window. . .once, twice. I hear that. His eyes find mine and they want to know what I'm doing way up there. . .

TALLER somehow.

There is surprise on his face

And blood. . .his and mine

His head smacks the window

one more time

and

I

STOP.

CHAPTER FORTY-THREE

As I pant and gasp to catch up with my breathing, my brain is a hummingbird, like I'm in the middle of one of those music videos where all the things are coming at you from all different angles one after the other but you can't really focus on anything—bap, bap, bap. . .

"You boys settle down back there," the substitute bus driver says. I barely hear under my own jackhammer gasps, but see her grey eyes in the rearview.

Bap. People standing and cheering. Still.

Bap. Big bus driver eyes in the rearview.

Bap. Blood. From Robert's head? Is that real?

Bap. High fives.

Bap: Me thinking all my thoughts: Did we just have a fight? Who were they rooting for? Did I WIN? If I won, what do I get? And. . .did I just stop? Why? Bap-bap-bap-bap—can't breathe.

I don't want to turn around. Part of me wants to, you know, like animals do after they kill another animal; kind of nudge it around a little bit before eating a chunk of it. Or like in the movie Mrs. Rubin showed us where the SS would shoot you in the middle of your head, blood pouring out of one hole in your skull like water from a smooth running spigot. Then another SS would bend down and snap off your cavity fillings from your dead teeth. No. I will just look outside and take my ride, like Jews used to have to do: Watch someone you know get shot, but then still have to board the train and roll on. If not, that's because it's you down there, losing your fillings.

Bap. Bus driver's eyeballs. Grey hair. No tattoos.

I hear my breath ticking inside my eardrums. Everything is slowing down as my breathing finally hums to a low roar and I'm having trouble knowing what's real or not real. There are all these pictures and sounds that are happening, but it's all behind me and I can't turn around.

Are Devon and some other kids acting as if Robert Bullock just won the fight? Wait, he didn't even punch me back. Devon says, "He got a few good ones in, Robert. Pretty scary."

Another kid says, "I'd be poundin' on that shrimp."

Another kid says, "I don't know, man, that little dude put on a show."

Robert says, "Check out Ratner's face. I dotted that eye."

Devon says to Bullock, "Is that blood on your shirt?"

"Where?"

"Right here," Devon says, pointing. And then, with a hint of amazement and concern, Devon says, "Dude, your head's bleeding."

God.

I feel sick.

CHAPTER FORTY-FOUR

The elevator is broken, but I need to get there. My breath is still ticking in my ears and my head is on fire.

Before I arrived here, I went home, but I did not go *in* my house. I did not pass GO and did not collect $200 for finally beating Robert Bullock. No. I just grabbed my bike and the unfolded stack of newspapers for my route, and rode 100 mph to the Regency Towers.

I throw up in the stairwell between Floor 9 and floor 10.

And again at floor 14 (there is no 13). Puking. Heaving. Puking up water now.

I keep going up. My breathing gets all amped again, pounding in my throat, and my head aches too much to figure out how to get my own heartbeat back beating in my heart again instead of in my Adam's apple.

On floor 15, I stop and look at the number 15 and the number gets blurry for a second, and then the one and five look exactly like the bus driver's eyeballs. I close my eyes and shake the eyeballs off of my brain. Then I puke again, spraying the wall underneath the numbers.

The biggest moment of my life so far, and I should be feeling happy for finally "accomplishing" this tremendous feat – I beat the *giant*. But I can't get my body to settle down and pay attention to the news of what we, me and my body, did. My body is betraying me. Instead of being happy, it's not even the opposite of happy, which would be sad. It's the opposite of well or sane. . . it's just sick. God, what's wrong with me?

I am on the roof of the Regency Towers, and I'm about to let go and fly.

Just want to lean over, drop, soar, shut my head off.

Sara Rothman will understand. She will be the only one. Maybe my sister will give her the letters, all 15 of them.

I reach down to undo the strap that holds the stack of newspapers, and for the first time since I was on the bus, I see my hands:

Blood.

On my fingers and both palms. Dried. Smeared. On my fingernail of the pointer finger. Inside, between the finger and nail. Some splashed across the top of my hand.

I spit into my palms. Again. Wash my hands with my own spit, rub hard to get the blood off of me.

My top two knuckles have it dried and caked on them. They are cut, that's why. I'm not sure whose blood is in there.

I mash my hands down into a little puddle of leftover rain in the divot behind me, soaking up all the muddy water. It feels dirty and good. I get most of it out, except for the blood in between my fingernail and my finger. And the blood deep in my cut knuckles thins but doesn't disappear. No spit or puddle is gonna make this go away.

I push the pile of newspapers all the way to the edge of the roof and step on top of the stack. I've never been this high before. I look down and a jolt of electricity rushes up my body. My toes take it in. Shooting up through my groin, the current lands in my belly and stays there. I can see all of Cherry Hill – all the pools in the backyards and all of the fences that surround them. But no matter how high in the sky I am, I can't seem to get the sound of Robert's head hitting the back window out of my head.

The sound of the air is hurting my ears too; echoes like Robert Bullock's breath when I was punching him. I want to tell Robert we need to stop all of this because a train is coming and they are going to stuff us both in the same windowless cattle car and lock the door from the inside. Will he still flick my ears?

Off to the camps we will go. I can hear it. I can smell it.

Urine. No. Piss. And crap. All the crap people can't hold in.

I am on the roof.

I can't take it; this feeling I have inside of me is *electricity*. I'm having trouble finding a place for myself. And when I throw up again, it's voltage rising from my stomach, coating my throat, into the air, splattering the roof floor.

The current pulsing in my belly is telling me it wants more electricity.

I could do it.

I want to.

So that it's over.

Just. . .

Let

Go

And

Fly.

CHAPTER FORTY-FIVE

The sun is big, on top of me, a giant lid about to clamp shut over my entire body.

The only thing I will say, for the record, is that I'm not into vampires or zombies. But I'm also not making this up either: Jackson McCaffery from the old neighborhood is here – I swear – and he pushed me back off the newspaper stacks right before I was going to jump into the sky.

That is what happened, even though nobody will believe me, so I'm not going to say it. Has to be. It's definitely NOT because I started thinking. THINKING. Because I can't be *that* broken. I mean, Robert Bullock isn't sitting at home feeling awful about me. Boiling sick with electricity. It's not because I started thinking about that movie Mrs. Rubin showed us. And it's not because I was thinking about Sara and her family moving to the Middle East to help people on both sides of a giant wall stop fighting each other so they could live better. I was NOT thinking all these guilty thoughts just like the guilty Jewish BOY my mom raised me to be. A real man just jumps, right? Which is what I was doing before Jackson McCaffery – dead Jackson McCaffery – pushed me back.

I swear, Jackson McCaffery is now blotting out part of the sun's blinding light, walking toward me. It's hard to see because of the sun's glare, but it's him. He's limping and bleeding. A lot. Like he just got run over by that hatchback one minute ago because all the blood is still fresh and oozing, his right leg mangled. I know this can't be happening, right? Serious.

"Jack?" I ask, and somehow scramble to a standing position.

It's also weird because Jack *used* to be taller than me, way taller.

I guess, maybe, I did grow? And Jack didn't?

He waddles back to the edge of the roof, peers out, not blinking at all. Apparently the sun doesn't bother dead people.

"The old neighborhood?" I swear Jack McCaffery says this, limping my way.

"Yeah?" I say, moving out of his way as he steps onto the edge of the roof.

"It's old," he says. I'm not making this up.

"So?" Makes me angry, hearing him say that. Plus, I mean, you come here all dead and mangled, and that's what you have to say to me?

He spreads his arms out, like wings – dead wings – bends, and then he leaps, seriously, diving into a pool of clouds.

I instinctively run to the edge of the roof, leap up onto my newspapers again, and I yell for him, for Jack, to save my dead friend from killing himself.

I swear it was him—is him—and now he's disappeared. Again. Gone. Like poof, gone. The sky is empty except for the gigantic sun, so close. . .so close—

"Larry!" I hear someone call behind me. It's Kevin, huffing and puffing out of breath, all urgent and serious. "Don't jump! Don't, man!"

It's shocking to hear Kevin call after me, and instead of reaching for the sun, I'm flapping my arms to keep from "accidentally" falling over the edge. Kevin staggers closer to me, not sure whether to run or proceed with caution.

I steadily step down from the stack, and for the first time, I catch a glimpse of the huge headline scrawled across the front page below me: ISRAEL STRIKES BACK. It's weird because our local paper doesn't typically feature any world news. More like when the next PTA bake sale is, or that Joe the dentist bowls a perfect game. It's also strange, of course, because Sara Rothman lives in Israel. With her people, who are my people too, I guess. So, really, OUR people struck back. And an hour ago, on the bus, I struck back too: My people struck back against. . .my people.

"I heard about you and Bullock," Kevin says, a sense of relief in his voice, because I didn't jump off the roof I guess, and also trying to sound like this is just a normal conversation between *friends*. But. . .what the hell is he doing here?

"Yeah, well," I say, pissed, trying to sound like a total jerk. "Whoever said something probably lied. Everybody lies about what happens."

"Yeah, well. . ." Kevin says, nodding at my hands. "Blood don't lie."

Hearing that makes me shudder. I glare at him and shove my hands in my pockets. He looks at me all crazy. He wants me to say something, but no way.

"Robert Bullock can't ball for nothin' anyway, you feel me?" he says. "Coach just liked him 'cause he's tall. Shoot, you got more game in your little finger than Robert Bullock. Bein' tall's one thing, but bein' a baller, you know. . . just 'cause you're tall don't mean you can handle your bid-ness, you know what I sayin'?"

I do. And I don't need to be sayin' I do, so I pretty much clam up. It's easy to say if you're actually tall and some algebra teacher/fake coach looks you in your eyes instead of down at you. But I ain't saying jack, and neither is Kevin. He just kicks a stone across the roof, then another, and another, and whatever.

"About Monica, man," Kevin finally says.

"Look, it's like, you know?" And the electricity is back, all back. "I don't wanna be thinking about Monica Johnson. I mean, c'mon." And I don't. Sara Rothman is who I like to think about when I think about a girl. Not Monica in her perfect jeans with her giggly sister and all of it.

See, that's the problem with me. I never wanted to kick Kevin's butt after he danced with Monica right in front of me. I just wished I never knew him or played ball with him or wanted to be like him. But now, all of a sudden, I want to punch him, even though he could kick my ass all over this roof, even though there's no one here to pull me off of him or him off of me. This electricity makes me want to go right through him. Maybe blood *does* lie, or at least takes its time telling the real truth. Because maybe I'm exactly like my father after all and that's why my body is so sick with this strange voltage. "I gotta go—"

"She kept calling me at home," Kevin says, all serious. Almost whiny.

"What?" I say, staring in his eyes, clenching my fist. Now I wanna hear.

"Yeah. She did. But. . .I shoulda told her no, no thank you, and I thought about that, you know? But then she comes up to me smellin' all like vanilla, asking me to ask her. Man, I just couldn't think straight."

While Kevin talks, the current grows and swirls in my gut, the same jolt from right before I hit Bullock, and from just before Jackson McCaffery saved me from jumping. This electricity! Impossible to control myself, like somebody else is pushing all the buttons in my brain. Man!

I'm not sure, but I think I yell, or yelp, I don't know, but I snap the rope around the newspaper stack. I grab the first section of the top newspaper and hang it over the edge until it screams in the breeze. Then I let go. The cold wind takes it slowly down and around and down some more, a beautiful ride, spiraling 26 floors of sky.

Then I violently crumple the next section and the next and the next until I get to the next newspaper and I smash all of it into dozens of newspapers balls, and start throwing ball after ball as hard as I can, like throwing a runner out at home plate from right field, showering the Cherry Hill sky with every last piece.

"Larry!" Kevin says, half trying to stop me, and half, I imagine, really impressed. "You're gonna get so fired," he finally says, as I throw and throw.

"So?" I crumple the last paper. "You heard the rabbi. I'm a man now."

Doing this: seeing newspapers float with the greatest of ease in the Jersey sky makes my belly simmer down and I feel a sliver of happiness. I almost feel tall, and like Kevin is actually looking up at me.

"So, what was it like?" Kevin asks. "Poundin' on punk-ass Bullock?"

"What do you mean?" I say, throwing the horoscope page. "You know."

Kevin nods. "Nope," he says. "Never been in a fight, believe it or not."

"What?" I say, stopping mid-throw. I can't believe what I just heard.

"Nobody messes with me," he says. "I would fight. Just looks painful is all."

How can you be the toughest kid in the school without ever getting into a fight? You just be tall and go around and talk like a girl so everyone laughs at your jokes. That's how. Insane. Just because you have a tall mom and a tall dad, you get to be on the basketball team and people don't want to fight you and girls who wear really tight jeans want to dance with you. It almost makes me start laughing right here on the roof.

It's only when I catch a glimpse of my cut knuckles and think about Robert Bullock dancing at my bar mitzvah, and then his head smacking against the back window, his candy cane teeth. . . I start to wish I could still fly away.

But I'm not. I'm sticking around. Just not here. "I gotta go," I say and leave Kevin on the roof, because I know what to do – not gonna think twice about it.

Chapter Forty-Six

I dart upstairs, past Marna who is yelling at me to stop, but no way am I stopping, no way, I have to do this now or I won't ever do it. No more thinking, just doing.

"Larry, wait," Marna calls after me.

I grab every letter I wrote to Sara Rothman, all 15 of them, race down the stairs past Marna again, who keeps calling after me to stop, but I don't, nope, I jump over the last four stairs, out the front door, and sprint down our driveway, snatch the stack of mail that's already in our mailbox, replace it with my stack, and flip up the little red flag.

Sara Rothman may move back to Cherry Hill or she may stay in Israel, I don't know. She may live on the moon; she's that amazing. I don't know if I'll ever see her again. Ever. Or maybe she'll move back here and she'll see me and decide I'm not cool enough or tall enough or whatever enough. It doesn't matter. I mean, it matters, but I can't let any of it stop me. I wrote 15 letters to Sara Rothman, all of them about the real me, talking to the real her, and never sent any of them. Today, no matter what, I'm sending them all.

Done. Red flag up: 15 letters on their way to the Middle East.

I look down at the mail in my hands, and on top, I can't even believe it, another letter for me with an Israel return address. It's got to be from Sara, maybe saying she's coming home for sure, and maybe she wants to see me right away. Damn, just seeing the Hebrew hieroglyphics gets my heart revved up again, but this time in the best way possible. I'm loving the rush, and don't really hear my sister.

"Larry, wait!" She screams, jarring me out of my trance. I swear.

"I got another letter," I say, trying not to smile. "Look." Marna is crying.

She's holding one of today's extra newspapers, the headline ISRAEL STRIKES BACK almost screams at me now above the huge picture of an explosion that covers most of the front page. If you didn't know better, it looks like today's section is really just Fourth of July coverage.

"She's dead, Larry," Marna says, holding up the newspaper to show me. She points to the small article below the giant explosion photo.

"Who is?" I ask, still sort of hyperventilating.

She nods to the envelope in my right hand, then holding the paper up to my face, points to the four paragraphs under the horrific picture in her hands.

I read it. . .again and again and one more time before. . .

"It's been on the news too," Marna says. "And Twitter and all of it."

I think my legs start to wobble, I think that's what happens. I know I drop all of the mail from my left hand, and it smacks onto the driveway.

I'd like to say I held onto the one piece of mail in my right hand, but I don't really know for sure.

And then everything that was light, the sunny day, all of it, becomes total darkness, and all of a sudden I'm staring at the Cherry Hill sky, again, until the next moment when even the sky disappears.

CHAPTER FORTY-SEVEN

When I wake up, I'm in my bed, with Sara's letter sitting on my chest.

My parents and sister are here telling me I'm okay, that I just passed out for a little while. Before I can utter a word, they make me chug loads of water, claiming I'm dehydrated. My mom gives me two Tylenol and puts a cold washcloth on my forehead like she used to do when I'd get migraines, and another one over my still-swollen eye.

"I'm getting you more water, Mister," my mom says, all worried.

"Water," my dad says, sorta goofy. Maybe he might go back to being my dad finally. "Water good for you," he adds, like he's an Indian war chief.

"Then you can tell us all about the blood." My mom points to my hands and shirt.

Once my parents leave, Marna, who rarely spends more than a second in my room, let alone off the phone, is, well, lingering.

Her eyes get all glassy, and her face starts dripping with tears again. This is so NOT Marna. She never cries, let alone twice in one day. As the world is coming into focus again, I remember: Sara's. . .dead.

But that's not exactly why she's crying.

"I wrote that letter," Marna says. "You know, from her, the first one."

"What?" I say, sitting up, the cool washcloth dropping to my lap.

"I know, I know, I'm sorry, I'm sorry," she says, crying more. "I wasn't trying to trick you – I mean, I was sort of – but really I just wanted you to *have* something. Something I knew you needed. You wrote 15 letters to this girl and you never sent even one. Who does that? Who does that, Larry?"

I fall back on my pillow, head throbbing, and stare at the ceiling.

"I read your letters you wrote to her. Very easy to do if you just sort of unfasten them with hot steam from a pot of boiling water. . .I've seen it on YouTube."

"*You* wrote it?" I ask, not even angry, more like it's dawning on me that Sara didn't really say what I thought she said and it's hitting me like a ton of Israeli missiles, exploding my heart into shreds of shrapnel.

She nods. "But not the picture she drew. That's hers. I got that off of her Facebook page. From your Facebook account. So, yeah. She's quite the artist, and she does draw in her bomb shelter. Which is creepy, but hey, we love who we love."

"Yeah, well, she doesn't draw jack anymore, does she?" I say, wanting to sound annoyed, but the words lump in my throat.

My sister nods, turns away, wiping her face, cleaning up her whole crying act, and sits next to me on my bed.

"I'm sorry, Larry," she says, grabbing my hand. "I knew you needed someone to love on you, someone you clearly loved back, because I could tell you were dying. . .and that you needed some. . .some magic."

I don't even know what to say, and honestly, as angry as I should be, I feel so weak, achy and confused, it's not in me to do something to Marna. What would I do?

And then she says as soft and as genuine as I've ever heard Marna say anything, "Larry, that one," she points to the letter in my hand, the new one, the unopened one from the mailbox before I passed out, "is real. I swear. It's her."

Two things land on me, and as hard as I try, I can't push them off. One, Marna is telling the truth. You can never tell when Marna is telling the truth or not, except for today, right now, when she is. And two, Sara Rothman is dead.

"I can't," I say. "She's. . ." And I can't even say it because it's stuck now in my chest; it didn't even make it to my throat. The thought of reading this letter right here and right now would hurt more because I would know Sara really wrote it, which means she had to be alive to write it. And now she isn't.

I look at the letter in my hand: my hand that still has all the ruins of the day stuck to it – blood and newspaper ink. The paper that tells the story of Sara's death, the paper that I threw off the roof. . .instead of me. According to the article, when Israel struck back with missiles and bombs or whatever the heck explodes and kills people on the other side of the wall at Gaza, Sara Rothman happened to be on that side of the wall. Reports say that her "friends" actually dug a tunnel from one side of the wall to the other. Serious. Like kids in a giant sandbox, digging. Not to transport explosives or smuggle fugitives or spies or weapons or whatever. Just to meet. Just to play. Like Sara said she wanted.

But it just so happened to be Israel's turn to "strike back," after Palestinians had struck back after Israel struck back after Palestinians had struck back. . . and so on and so on. It never stops. As Mrs. Rubin always says when she talks about Gaza, who knows which came first, the chicken or the egg?

It makes me think maybe I'm not like my dad after all. It's coming back to me – the whole "fight" on the bus – I stopped. Nobody pulled me off. *I* stopped. Maybe because whatever started me, whatever we think makes up who we are – my dad or my mom, or even Marna – my *blood*, suddenly wasn't there anymore. It was just me. I think I stopped because somebody had to. Or else. . .somebody is always *striking* back and we just end up hurting our own people. And it never ends. Because sometimes, nobody does pull you off; nobody steps up and stops the fight.

Or worse, maybe I stopped because I started *thinking*. Maybe, for once, I actually stopped thinking and just reacted and it was good. . .and 100% human to do. And then, I went back to being ME and started thinking too much and that's why I stopped.

My mom returns and hands me a giant glass of water. "Okay, 'fess up," she says, lifting my hands up. "Blood. Truth, please."

I pull my hands away. "I fell," I say. "At Regency Towers, while I was doing my route." Which is true. Even though it's really a lie. But the truth is stuck in my chest.

My mom gives a worried sigh, not really believing me, but not willing to chase it. "So, you know this girl?" she says. "The one that died by friendly fire who's from here?"

Friendly fire. Huh. Interesting phrase we use to describe how we hurt or kill our own people. The friendly part means we didn't mean to, I guess.

Part of me wants to tell my mom everything about how I know this girl, but all of that gets stuck in my chest too. I don't know why. My dad is the teacher in the house, but my mom has taught me all the important stuff: how to tie my shoes, to brush my teeth, to put on deodorant, to match my clothes properly, to open doors for girls, when to get a haircut, where to put my hands when I slow dance (I didn't ask, she just showed me, which was embarrassing), and that it's your family, your blood, that's always there for you no matter what. But. . .I don't *know* Sara, really. Do I? I just danced with her once.

"He had a crush on her," Marna says, soft and real. But she's lying.

"No," I say, and look at Marna hard, shaking a little. "I loved—love her."

"Wait, what?" my mom asks. Shocked. Marna lights up.

"She was my only friend," I say, wiping my face with my forearm and stuffing the envelope under my pillow. "You invited her to my bar mitzvah."

Chapter Forty-Eight

I t's 2:52 in the morning, but I can't sleep anymore. I pretty much fell asleep after my mom brought me another giant mug of water, before the sun set; my body just couldn't stay awake anymore. Now, out my window, it's pitcher-than-pitch black – gloomy, like the sky is a giant secret everyone else is sleeping through.

And my body is so, I don't even know. . .broken? I'm more than achy. My muscles are more than sore, my throat more than dry, stomach more than empty, and my head is more than throbbing. I need to just go back to sleep, clearly.

But the envelope under my pillow is this giant ticking thing.

I wake up Marna, who is wearing her retainer headgear, snoring, drooling, and hugging her cell phone, I swear. It's 3 a.m., but I need her.

She wipes the sleep from her eyes with her knuckles, like a little kid and not a girl about to live with her boyfriend in apartment 2B. If you wear a headgear, you should have to live with your original family until your teeth are all-the-way straight. That should just be a rule.

When she fully focuses, she sees the envelope I'm holding in front of her face. She sits up quick, her back against her headboard, and nods at the letter in my hands.

"Go ahead," she says as gentle as Marna can be. "You can do it. I'm here."

I start to speak, but the words get stuck as if I hadn't uttered a word in 50 years. I clear my throat and say, "And you promise you didn't write this?"

Marna places both hands over her heart and says, "Girl Scouts honor."

We both almost laugh. It's crazy because it feels like Marna is reading my mind two steps before I think what I think, knowing I don't all-the-way believe her. Like a cat, she leaps from her bed and darts out of her room. She's back in literally two seconds, and from behind her back pulls out the envelope from the first letter and holds the two letters side by side and nods for me to look. The first one just has a stamp-sized sticker with Hebrew letters on a regular envelope. The second has a real Israel stamp on an airmail envelope, with three real squiggly lines through the stamp because that's what the post office does right before they really mail something. Because this letter is really real.

We stare at each other, like we're making a deal to take over the world. Marna can be so frighteningly intense, it's, well, intense.

And then, without taking my eyes off of her, I open the letter. Marna nods at me to unfold it, and I turn away to read the letter to myself:

Dear Larry - Shalom from this side of the world and from this side of the Wall. Ha! That's a Gaza joke ☺

Can I tell you that I JUST read your letter for the millionth time? You are a good writer, Larry. I knew that last year (remember the class where you never talked to me? ☺) when you'd write stories, even though you never read them out loud during Open Mic days. I always peeked.

You shouldn't be scared to read your stuff out loud, Larry. Honest.

Great news. . . There's a more than 70% chance we are moving back to Cherry Hill this summer! I want to see you - you most of all. And I know you grew taller, Larry, so don't even go there. Though it doesn't matter to me anyway. I mean, I have friends here I've never actually seen (though I hope to soon!). So who cares how tall somebody is?

I want to say one more thing and then I have to go to school, but Robert Bullock thinks he's all that; he isn't. He's just tall, and that ain't much. But, don't fight him! Nothing ever gets solved that way. Hello? Watch the world news, look at the Middle East coverage, and you'll see how stupid really smart people can be. Plus, you're both Jewish. And Jews can't be fighting other Jews. Not in this world. There's just not enough of us to go around, trust me. So don't fight him, Larry. Okay? You're "bigger" than that! I mean it.

And one more thing. No, two. One is, please send me more letters! I love your letters. And two, well, ah, oh, ah, ah. . .I like you too. A lot.

Love always,

Sara

I look up. I'm crying, like Marna was earlier, rain dripping down my face, and Marna is smiling because she knows when someone reads a love letter.

We're not the kind of siblings who hug each other at all, not one bit, but by the time I finish Sara's letter, my body suddenly loses all its bones or something. I wouldn't say Marna reached out to hug me, more like she reached out to catch my crumpling skeleton and now we happen to be hugging.

"You sent my—" I can't even talk.

AARON LEVY

"Just the one," she says. "The last one. Well, you wrote 'burn this' on it, so I followed the directions and burned it – well, um, steamed it open. That's when I knew the letter had to get in the appropriate hands or else. . .I don't know, God would destroy something."

God *did* destroy something. Sara. Even if he didn't mean to.

And once again, I'm totally sad and totally happy at the same time. Serious. The low simmer of electricity that's been sitting in my gut, leftover from this day, is gone. Sara Rothman likes me. And. . .I believe her.

CHAPTER FORTY-NINE

My parents let me sleep in instead of getting up for school. Plus, I told them I did not want to attend the school-wide memorial assembly being held in the gym for Sara. Strangely, my parents were pretty cool about agreeing with me and not asking a ton of questions about why I didn't want to go.

The news stations will apparently be covering the event. They are making a big deal about the loss of Sara Rothman, even though her family is still in Israel and refuses to speak to anyone. It's so weird, because nobody paid attention to Sara when she was going to school, except for her small boobs, right, or when her family left Cherry Hill to help in Israel. But now she's famous. My dad quoted some song I don't know, ". . .people love you when they know you're leaving soon. . ." I think that's true, and also really sad.

Which is why I don't want to be around a bunch of people who didn't really know her. I'm sure there will be a bunch of crying teachers too. I remember Mr. Marciano backstage with our whole class, and that kind of freaked me out, and he actually knew Jack. But I don't want to sit in a circle holding hands with people I don't really know and cry all in public. Or feel like a jerk for not crying all in public.

I finally wake up and stumble into the shower, but it doesn't make me feel any better. I'm weak and achy everywhere. I probably need some nourishment, but my stomach is saying, "Uh-uh, closed for business."

When I stumble downstairs and sort of fall into a kitchen chair, my mom greets me with her hands on her hips and says, "Where is she?"

Unfortunately, when my sister left for school today, she didn't go to school either. And since my parents are both unemployed, they were home to receive the call from the attendance office announcing Marna was absent today, and that she's been absent more than six days this semester. Then my mom also fields a call from Mrs. Smith saying Marna hasn't been to Girl Scouts in months and can she hand in her final cookie money.

"It's our fault," my mom says, sort of staring out the window at nothing. "We give and give and give and this is the thanks we get. Fools."

I could add to all of their parenting joy and warn them to be on the lookout for another phone call – the one firing me from my paper route, but that will be a surprise for all of us coming soon enough.

Or I could speak up and say, "Guess what? I beat up Robert Bullock yesterday, I think. Aren't you proud of me?" But the thought of that announcement making anyone feel better makes the electricity in my gut stir.

"Please, Larry," my dad says, gentle but despairing. "I'd really like to retrieve my daughter from wherever she might be."

I look at my mom and my dad. They're nervous, sure, but they also seem really desperate. My body is exhausted. Simply, I've got no more fight in me and am about to just give in. At the same time, I promised Marna that I wouldn't tell. But then why did she take me to Bucky's in the first place? She could have told me all that stuff without showing me his apartment. And now she puts me in this predicament. The same sibling who wrote me a fake letter from Israel.

"There might be one place—"

"Let's go," my mom says, ushering me to get back into the car. It's like I'm being kidnapped by the mob and taken to the bridge where they'll dispose of me.

I take a step to get into the car and sort of stumble I guess.

"Whoa," she says. "Are you okay?"

"I'm fine," I say, trying to get around her.

"You don't look so good." She immediately pushes the back of her hand against my forehead like mothers do. "You're burning up."

"I'm not. Hot shower," I lie, ducking into the car. "That's why. I'm fine." I give my dad directions from the back seat. While we're on Kressen Road, going uphill, I just pop the question because I don't care anymore and I'm going to ask what I wanna ask. I say boldly, "Are we moving to Las Vegas?"

In sync, my mom: "No." My dad: "Yes." I want to say, "Somebody is a liar," but I don't, because suddenly, we're here.

"There," I say, pointing. "2B. That's Bucky's apartment."

"Who's Bucky?" They ask in unison. Hmm. I don't even know. The guy who maybe does nasty things with my sister when she should be at school or Girl Scouts?

"He's Jewish," I say, trying my best to answer the question. I feel really nervous for Marna too. My breathing returns immediately to my throat again.

"This is what she does? Skips school to gallivant with, with Buck?"

"Alls I know is that he's Jewish," I say, stomach gurgling. "I think."

"Go get her, Dan," my mom says. He undoes his seatbelt and clears his throat the way he always does before he gets up off the couch when my mom orders him to do something like take out the trash, or change a light bulb, or go discipline the children.

But just as my dad is about to knock on the door, we hear a scream that sounds like Marna and then a big "OUUUUUUCH!" that sounds like Bucky. The door flies open and Bucky bolts out, Marna racing behind him, only Bucky is holding his nose and blood is pouring out of it. My dad jumps back to the side involuntarily, getting out of the way.

"Wait! Wait! I'm sorry!" Marna screams. My mom flies out of the car faster than she's really capable of moving. Bucky is trying to open his car door, but he's having trouble manipulating the keys, and he's saying "my nose" over and over as if it's fallen off his face and is rolling down the street. Marna stops dead in the middle of the parking lot when she suddenly realizes that my mom and dad are in fact *here*. One nanosecond later, she spots me in the back seat of the car. I lock the door.

She looks at my mom and then at my dad and then bolts for me. "Why, you! I can't believe you told them!" She's pulling the door handle and banging on the window.

Everybody is talking at once:

My mom is saying, "This is what you do instead of going to school?!!"

I'm saying, "They made me do it!"

Bucky is saying, "Ow!" and "Jeez!" and "She broke my nose!"

Marna is saying, "I'm going to kill you!"

My mom is now saying, "This is who you are now?!"

My dad doesn't know if he should break Bucky in half or help him out. Then he takes out his handkerchief and walks over to Bucky, who looks at my dad, then at Marna, and finally takes the handkerchief. "Put your head back. . .like this," my dad says. They both now have their heads back. "That's it. Squeeze the middle of your nose, like this, and put your head back, like this. That's it. Now, c'mon."

With his head now back, handkerchief plugging up his bleeding nostrils, Bucky says, "Bucky, sir. It's real nice to meet you. Marna sure talks about you a lot."

Everyone finally stops talking. Bucky continues to bleed. A lot.

"Ah, Susan?" my dad interrupts. When he says my mom's name instead of Sue or Honey Muffin, it's pretty serious. "This boy needs some medical attention pronto."

My mom looks at Marna and then at Bucky – Marna-Bucky-Marna-Bucky. . .and then orders everybody into the car. We're either going to the hospital or to throw somebody off the bridge. It could be Bucky or Marna or both. Or me. I'm an accomplice.

Bucky tries to introduce himself again, "Hello, Mr. and Mrs. Ratner. I just want to say it's completely a pleasure and an honor to meet you." He offers his hand to shake. Both my mom and dad kind of look at Bucky's bloody paw and then so does Bucky and he gives an "oh" and returns his hand back to his gushing nose.

"Keep your head back, son," my dad says. He was a nurse in the Army Reserves for two years before he ever became a teacher. He knows how to manage a bloody nose.

"Bucky, how do you skip school and have your own apartment?" my mom asks.

Bucky answers with his head back, sounding all nasally, "Well, Mrs. Ratner, I graduated from high school three years ago and now have a job watching out for foster kids at the group home in Marlton."

"Ah-huh," my mom says. "Already graduated high school. Three years ago."

Everybody's quiet. I think we're waiting for my mom to go off. I can see she's trying to hold it back, as she considers it's not socially appropriate to go off on your daughter in front of her friend. . .her older friend. . .her older boyfriend. . .the one she skips school with to hang out in his apartment . . .3. . .2. . .1!

"I'm disgusted," my mom says.

"Not now, mom," Marna spits back right away.

"I have complete and total respect for your daughter, ma'am," says Bucky, but you can hardly make out what he says. He sounds like a big nostril.

My mom doesn't hear any of it anyway because the rant is on: "Is this what we raised? Someone who sleeps around—"

"Sleeps around?!" Marna says, dumbfounded, on the edge of throwing a tantrum. "That's not what I was doing, but you only hear what you wanna hear—"

"Liar!" My mom yells. "You lied every time you walked out the door. Well, I hope it was worth it, Sweetheart. I hope you got your rocks off, sister, because the fireworks are over!"

"I love him!" my sister screams, slobber spraying from her mouth, like a toddler fighting for a toy in a sandbox. My mom throws up her hands in disgust. The whole car is silent. The only thing we can hear are the snorts from Bucky's oozing nose.

Blood is all over his shirt and face and now the back seat. He finally pipes up after what feels like years of silence, "Excuse me, ma'am and Mr. Ratner, ah sir, ah, do you have another snot rag or, or, or a simple tissue?"

Marna interrupts him, "Don't say *tissue*, that's so lame."

"Sorry," Bucky says. He is really uncool right now because everything he says sounds like a giant nose is talking.

Without looking, my mom tosses a box of Kleenex over her shoulder.

It hits Bucky square in the nose. "Whoa, Ouch!"

"Don't say *ouch* either," my sister snaps. "Man up, yo. Jeez."

"Sorry," Bucky says to Marna. "Thank you, Mrs. Ratner."

CHAPTER FIFTY

They take Bucky right away at the hospital because he is leaving a trail of blood everywhere. Marna tries to go back with him, but Bucky says, "You stay away from me."

"Okay," she says sort of smiley for her and everyone in the lobby, but I can tell it hurts her. "I'll just watch your jacket here."

My mom and dad help Bucky complete the paperwork with the nurse at the desk because when he tries to write, his nose gushes blood all over the forms. Marna reaches into Bucky's jacket, pulls out a pack of cigarettes and a lighter, and goes out to the curb in front of the emergency room.

And she lights up. My sister, it would appear, is a pro at smoking cigarettes now.

I go out there. "Marna, what are you doing? Put that out before Mom and Dad see it." Not to mention I'm pretty sure it's against the rules or law to smoke in front of an ER.

"You know what I like about hospitals?" she asks me, blowing out smoke into the parking lot. "You're there. Here. That's it. Boom. Go in, fix me, the end."

"They made me tell," I plead. She takes a giant drag from her smoke.

"We're in the hospital now, little brother. So, poof." She blows a fuller puff all in my face.

The emergency doors open just like all the doors do on the Starship Enterprise from Star Trek, and my parents walk out. They surround Marna, one on each side, and look at each other. Marna just keeps smoking. She's amazing. Crazy, but amazing.

"Dan, can you ask your daughter to extinguish her CIGARETTE before I shove it down her throat? Looks like she's picked up another one of your lovely habits."

My dad gently removes the cigarette from my sister's lips, and calmly squishes it into the pavement with the ball of his shoe like smokers do.

"Ask your daughter who on God's green earth she thinks she is."

So he does: "Who on God's green earth do you think you are?"

"Is she on drugs?" my mom asks my dad.

"Are you on drugs?" my dad asks Marna.

Marna snaps back, almost right through my dad, "Are you gonna make a scene? In the parking lot here? 'Cause we're already at the hospital. So. . .so, you know?"

"Your mother would like an answer," my dad says, exerting himself.

"No, I'm not on drugs. I started smoking two weeks ago when I found out we were moving to Vegas, and if you really must know. . ." Marna can't finish. She starts to get choked up, but sucks it back in and starts again, "And if you really must know that was my boyfriend, Bucky, and I *broke* his nose after he *broke up* with me."

"That's your *boyfriend* now?" my mom asks.

"He broke up with you?" I ask.

"He must be about 25 years old," my dad says.

Marna looks at my dad. "He's 21," she says. My dad clears his throat, the kind of clearing that says, *here we go.*

"He broke up with me after I told him I was moving in with him because my family was abandoning me, moving across the country. . .and. . .and. . ." Marna starts to lose it, crying right here in the parking lot. It's all coming out, snot, everything, and she's sort of trying to talk at the same time and I think what's really happening is she's hyperventilating. "He told me that. . .he didn't think it was such a good idea for us to see each other anymore. He was gonna tell me next week after prom, but then I asked him," and here Marna takes a big breath because she's almost choking on her own crying.

"Slow down, Speed Racer," my dad says.

This makes Marna cry even more, and more, and get angry at the same time, until she finally utters, "I told him that I'm not going to Las Vegas. I'm staying right here in Cherry Hill with you and he said, 'I think we should see other people, people our own age maybe,' and that's when I socked him in the nose!"

My mom looks at my dad, who realizes it's time to try to be useful, I suspect. "You can't just punch people because you don't like what they say," my dad says.

Marna sneers at him, and even though she's crying, it's almost like she stops for one second and in the coolest, coldest tone, she says, "Why not? It's what you do."

This stings my dad, I can tell. If he had a plug for all of his internal circuitry, Marna just pulled it out of the wall. If he were a hot air balloon, he'd fizzle to the ground.

The electricity starts to stir in my stomach again. Damn. Can't help it.

"But you really hurt him, Marna!" I yell. For some reason, I'm yelling at Marna, even though I'm not her parent. "You, you broke his nose. I mean, you can't—that's NOT okay!"

Marna abruptly stops crying, and her and my mom and my dad all look at me – suddenly I'm some crazy person breathing hard outside of the dang emergency room.

"I know," Marna says, whimpering, trying to breathe and not cry at the same time. "I. . .I got scared I think."

Which doesn't make sense. . . who hits someone in the nose just because they get scared? That's what animals do. They don't think it through; they sense danger and strike. Like Mrs. Rubin says – the Germans got terrified about their economy, and instead of dealing with it head-on, they chose scapegoats. She says, look what fear becomes.

That's why I kept thinking I'm broken because I'm the opposite. The main reason I didn't hit Robert sooner is because I THOUGHT too much. I kept thinking he's too big and what if nobody pulled him off of me and what if he really hurt me and what if everyone watched him beat the living snot out of me, everybody watching, because maybe if I was taller and bigger I could do it, but I'm not, and what if I just ignore him maybe he'll ignore me back and then I wouldn't have to try to hurt him or be hurt by him, and what if what if what if what iffffffffff??????????

The truth is, I was *scared* too, which is why I didn't hit Robert back all those times he deserved it, all those times my parents privately wished I would. And now I think. . . why should I have to? So I can be a man? Or an animal?

I guess I thought if I was going to be a real man then I wasn't allowed to get scared. A real man just takes care of his business. I'm not so sure anymore.

Marna is uncontrollable now, crying and gently heaving. Like she just saw the end of the world and had to talk about it. I don't know. I look at my mom who looks at my dad who taps me on the shoulder and motions for me to go with him.

We step back in the emergency room and leave my mom out there with Marna.

My dad and I watch from the window and see something I haven't seen in forever. My mom sits down on the curb next to Marna and puts her arm around her. Then Marna takes in a big breath and says in a sort of crying full-of-snot way, "Why doesn't he want me?" And with that, she buries her head into my mom, who just squeezes her tight and keeps saying that it is okay, while Marna cries it all out. I wonder if that's how it happened when we were babies and we were in terrible gas pain or something. Would my mom just hold us and say that it's okay? I can't remember any of it, but for some reason, it looks familiar.

I'm wondering too if you have to skip school, quit Girl Scouts, take up smoking, and break a 21-year old man's nose just to be able to really talk to my mom. But I also think it's the best thing I've seen all year. I wish I could talk to my mom about all this. But every time I think to do it, I just don't. Maybe because it won't change anything. It's weird, because in our old house, I used to talk to my mom about everything. Cartoons, my cousins, yucky girls, getting a dog, even when Jack died. Then we moved and everything kind of got bigger, and this stuff started to happen and I don't even know how to explain it.

Maybe my mom would be a good person to talk to about Sara Rothman, but. . .I don't know how to describe what she means to me, or could have meant to me. I'm just not good with words like that.

My mom is stroking the back of Marna's head. A bunch of people walk in and out, keeping the emergency doors open.

I hear Marna say, "You're not supposed to move a kid in the middle of high school, Mommy."

My mom says again, "Shhh, it's okay," over and over.

Wow.

My dad taps me on the shoulder and I jump. He smiles at me. "C'mon," he says. "Let's go visit your sister's new ex-boyfriend."

CHAPTER FIFTY-ONE

Except for his eyes and mouth, Bucky's whole face is bandaged up, and when my dad and I get to his room, he's trying to drink some orange juice through a straw but having great difficulty, I suppose, because he can't breathe through his nose. He doesn't get a private room, just a bed in some space behind a big shower curtain gizmo, attempting to make it private. But you can hear the woman "next door" complaining about how she doesn't do needles well.

"How are you doing, Buck?" my dad asks, as if they've known each other from my dad's old neighborhood. Jeez.

Bucky dribbles some orange juice down his gown they give you in hospitals. It's kind of weird to see Bucky like this, all bloody, bandaged, and mangled, because the last time I saw him was this summer when he was pretending to be an angry Nazi.

"Mr. Ratner," Bucky says, all nervous. "Hi, Sir, oh, yeah, we don't know yet. We're waiting for the doc to check me out. This wrap is just so I stop bleeding all over America. The nurse thinks I broke my nose in several places, though, which is odd because I didn't really know that a nose had bones to it, you know? I thought it was cartilage and nostril, ah, what – material? But then I'm not a nose-it-all." He tries to laugh, but then stops because it hurts too much. "Get it?" he smiles.

My dad sort of fake laughs at Bucky. He's always really good about making people feel funnier than they really are. "I broke my nose seven times before I was 18," my dad says. "Trust me, there's bones in this shnoz." And then my dad gets silent for a moment, and finally all serious, he says, "I'm real sorry about this, Bucky."

Bucky looks at him and then at me, and takes a slurp of OJ from his straw. "Look," he swallows and says, "I'm not gonna sue you if that's what you're worried about. But I'm just not as interested in dating your daughter anymore and I hope that's okay with everyone involved here."

"Yes, of course, that's your business," my dad says. "We weren't so worried about you suing us as we currently don't have jobs or material things, so it'd be somewhat futile. I did take care of your medical bill here though."

"Thank you, Sir, you didn't have to do that."

My dad says, "I was more concerned about the future of your face."

Bucky slurps some more OJ from his straw. He looks like a timid kindergartener.

"I'm waiting on the doc, as I mentioned," Bucky says almost a little irritated.

It's weird, because now I'm thinking Bucky is a nice guy and probably treated my sister really good. And he definitely didn't deserve to be wacked in the nose, or get introduced to my wonderful family during a bloody car ride to the hospital.

"Your daughter packs quite a right hook, ah, respectfully," Bucky says, putting his OJ on the tray. "You teach her how to fight, Sir?" Bucky looks at me, right at my swollen eye, which I'm sure he already knew about because Marna tells him everything. Or used to. It makes me self-conscious all of a sudden because, honestly, I forgot about my eye until just now. Now, my eye hurts and my face feels lop-sided. Serious.

My dad doesn't answer at first, but sort of backs away from Bucky's bed, toward the door. It's almost as if Bucky sucker punched him in the stomach, and now my dad seems lopsided too.

"I think I did," my dad finally says, all serious. He's talking to Bucky, my sister's new ex-boyfriend, but he's looking at me the whole time. "But I didn't mean to," he says, all weird and shaky and not my dad at all. . .because my dad, my father, who I've never seen cry, ever, is actually getting choked up.

There's a sudden rattle of the shower curtain gizmo that makes all of us jerk simultaneously, and we hear, "knock, knock," and then a short, bald guy wearing a white lab coat with a mask over his mouth and nose walks right past us to the clipboard hanging at the end of Bucky's bed. "I'm Dr. Spagnola," he says, picking up the clipboard. "Whoa, are you my patient too?" he asks me.

"What?" I say. Dr. Spagnola lets go of the clipboard with Bucky's file; it dangles from the bottom of his bed, and he points to my swollen eye. "No," I say, turning away.

I look over to my dad almost instinctively for some help with this adult person. This doctor. My dad's eyes are glassy and wet now, but he's suddenly super focused on looking at just me instead of greeting the doctor. Maybe he wants to respond to Dr. Spagnola, but I can tell he can't really talk right now, and all of a sudden I just want to save him instead. I don't even know.

"That's a big league shiner you got there," Dr. Spagnola says. "Are you his father?"

My dad nods.

"You know what happened there?" He asks, pointing.

My dad nods.

Dr. Spagnola sits and rolls over to me on his black wheelie chair and takes the pin light out of his front pocket on his lab coat. "Close your eye for me, wouldja?" I do it because I always do what doctors tell me to do when I'm in their house. "Yeah, that's not from any accidental fall or running into a door. That's a full-on knuckle sandwich. You can see the knuckle marks here, clear as day. See?" he asks my father while keeping his pin light focused on my eye, on the knuckle proof.

But my father sits still and doesn't come over to take a closer look like a concerned parent probably should or would, or like the doctor asked him to do. Dr. Spagnola turns away from my eye, and points his pin light at my dad.

"You do this?" he flat out asks him all matter-of-fact, like he's talking about the weather, or the Phillies.

"What?" my dad says, eyes still damp, his words grimy and stuck in his throat.

"Are you going to check my nose, Doc?" Bucky asks.

Dr. Spagnola gives Bucky the stiff arm like a running back or a traffic cop, indicating, "just one minute" but with his eyes focused squarely on my dad now.

"You know, by accident, some rough housing or what-not," Dr. Spagnola says. But then he pulls down his mask to just under his chin so we can all see his lips say the next thing, which he does slow and serious, punching every word, "Or maybe some discipline issue got out of hand? Hmm?"

Nobody says anything. My dad and Dr. Spagnola are staring at each other, but then my dad blinks, losing, and looks away. I don't know what to do. I've seen this scene on TV shows and they arrest people for this, right?

Bucky senses it as well, I think, and says, "Hello? Hi, doctor. Ah, excuse me, but are you able to check my nose to see if it's broken in several places? Sir?"

Dr. Spagnola points to Bucky's nose, but doesn't take his eyes off my dad. "You do that too?"

"What?" my dad asks again. He can't believe what's happening, I'm sure. I mean he's a teacher, an educator of young people. He's not some bruiser or molester or a drunk, or a. . . child abuser. My father doesn't need to go to jail. I mean, seriously.

"I got in a fight," I say out loud. Dr. Spagnola puts his pin light back in his pocket.

"Right," the doctor says, still looking at my dad accusingly.

"On the bus," I say, deeper. Louder. I make eye contact with Dr. Spagnola, just like my dad taught me to do. Eye contact.

"Is that what he told you to say?" he points at my dad.

"With Robert Bullock," I say louder and with more confidence. And then I raise my hands, and squeeze them into fists so that the doctor *and* my dad can see my cracked, scabbing knuckles. "He's a Jewish kid that's two feet taller than me and takes my bus and constantly sits by me and is always—he dropped his backpack on my head yesterday and it hurt like hell and my body got fed up I guess, so we got into a fight on the bus because maybe I stopped thinking and my body couldn't help it." My dad is shocked at what I'm saying out loud in this hospital, while I continue to hold my split knuckles up for all to see. I mean, he'd taught us to never lie. "I got in a fight on the bus," I say again.

Because I did.

CHAPTER FIFTY-TWO

Today is the first day my head isn't pounding, more like a dull ache, so me and Snowball are getting back out there to shoot hoops. I'm trying out for some basketball team next year, no matter where we live, no matter what, and even if I don't grow.

But on my way out the door, I find my mom in the kitchen, making pancakes, the smell of blueberry batter tickling my nose. When my mom is cooking us breakfast on the weekend, you know she's in a decent mood.

"I hope you're hungry, my man. I've got a million pancakes going here."

"I am." Even though I'm not, but I want to be. Normally, I'd just say no and go out and shoot. I don't know, just feels like I should stay and eat a pancake.

"Your father and sister are still sleeping. I guess your average *smoker* needs beauty rest," she says. She's definitely in a good mood. Normally she wouldn't say *smoker* so sing-songy. It's weird though, because there's one full place setting already on the table; a plate with a stack of pancakes, a glass of orange juice, napkin, and silverware.

"Mom?" I say.

"Yes, honey." She was about to flip a pancake high in the air and instead just flicks it over.

"If we move," I say, trying to figure out how to say what I want to say, but again, I'm not good with words. "I don't want it to be because it's hard for me here. I mean, it's like, I can, I can do it. I'll do better."

She clicks off the burner, and sets the spatula down carefully like a loaded weapon. "If we move, Larry, it's because there are teaching jobs for your father, in a district that doesn't go on strike, and a community we can afford. That's why. Because we Ratners may run into things – head on even – but we never run away from things."

"Okay," I say. "And, I can't believe I'm saying this, but, Marna has to move too."

My mom smiles. Weird. All of it's weird. The pancakes, the one lonely setting, and everything. "Where else would she go, Mister? She's part of this family."

She loads my plate with a stack of pancakes. "I'm just sayin'."

"C'mere," she says. My mom does something she doesn't normally do. . .she takes a knee. The last time was at my bar mitzvah when she was tying my bowtie and I remember thinking how she was still taller than me, even on her knees.

"In Las Vegas, everything is bright," she says, all intense. "Did you know that?" On the Strip, even McDonalds is lit up. You're not gonna believe how bright it will be."

And. . .for the first time ever, in the limited history of my mother taking a knee, I'm looking over her head. Serious.

"Mom," I say. "How come there's a full plate of pancakes set up?"

"Oh," she says, looking kind of crazy, UP into my eyes. "That's in honor of your *friend.* Sara." And that gets me suddenly choked. Just didn't see it coming. "Right?"

I nod and cover my eyes with both hands because I can't hold it.

She hugs me. "You're not gonna believe how bright it's gonna be," she whispers.

What I can't believe is how tight my mom's hug is, squeezing the snot out of my shoulders because that's where her hugs come to now. Because I actually got

TALLER. . .

I

GREW.

CHAPTER FIFTY-THREE

The next day, when I walk on the bus, the bus driver says, "How are ya doin', son?" It makes me freeze. I forget how to speak. "All right then, move it along," he says, and then he winks at me. Like he knows stuff.

Just as my heart stops racing from the bus driver talking to me, I see Heather sitting in a seat reading a book. Heather. On my bus. What? Oh no! I turn to get off the bus—she can't see me, not on the bus—when I hear, "Larry?"

"Heather?" I fake being surprised. "Wow. What are you doing here?"

And we say at the same time, "You take this bus?"

So we laugh because I guess that's what people do when they talk at the same time. She says, "Well, sit down maybe." I hesitate.

"You're not gonna get up and leave, are you?" I ask.

She smiles. Her whole face changes when she does. I didn't notice that before, maybe because she's sitting now and I'm looking down, or because we're not about to dance, but she looks pretty good. "No," she says. "I'm here to stay."

"I'd deserve it," I say in my best apologetic tone.

She nods, pats the seat, and I sit next to her. She smells like watermelon.

"Once a week, starting today, I go to my dad's house instead of my mom's," she says. "So I take this bus to get there."

Bullock is not here yet. Maybe he's taking the late bus. Please, God, put him on the late bus!

"Wow," I say, trying to look in her eyes. "That's, that's cool."

"Yeah, it's good for me to see him more than only once a week, you know," she says. "It's just different." I wish I knew what to say, but again, I'm lousy with words.

I'm looking at her in her eyes, really listening, until I hear my last name from the bus stairs. I pray to God. . .not today, not in front of Heather.

Bullock sees me now. I hope that he also sees me talking to Heather and just moves on, like some kind of man-code. But it makes me so nervous all of a sudden, talking to her. "But at least there's less arguing," I say, looking down and away but trying not to. "I hate when my parents go at each other."

"That's true," she says, gazing out the window. "It's not as noisy."

"Yeah, there's that," I say. Robert's coming up the steps now and I'm trying to ignore him and be here with Heather, but it feels impossible.

"Hey," she says. "That's pretty awful about Sara Rothman, huh?"

I want to say yes, but the words get stuck in my throat. Plus aside from being totally stressed out now, I'm instantly sad hearing Sara's name.

"I'm sorry," Heather says. "I didn't know her really. But I know she was your friend, so I'm sorry."

I nod and look out the window. Out of all the friends my age that are not my friends, Heather is right, Sara was my friend. And now she's gone.

Bullock looks right past me and sits with Devon, Toby, Jonathan and the rest of them about two rows back. Not far enough. I am listening to Heather talking, but now it's like I'm suddenly able to pick up an extra frequency.

"Look who it is," I hear Jonathan say to Robert.

"'Tsup," Robert says, not as loud as usual.

"I'm surprised you even came to school today after getting whooped on like that," Toby laughs and high-fives Jonathan.

"Please, did you see how I dotted that eye?" Robert says.

"Hey, man," I hear Devon pipe up, as if he's all concerned for Robert. It's like I hear all of this crystal clear and Heather hears none of it. She just watches the kids come out of school and walk like zombies to a million buses and talks to me about her family. If I could freeze Heather so that she'll never hear what's now in stereo in my ears, I would. "You gonna let that shrimp beat on you like that? Sucker punch you like that?"

"What are you talkin' about, man?" Robert is annoyed now and it's all my fault.

"No French fry like that is whoopin' on me," Devon says. "That's all I'm gonna say. No way."

"Yeah, yeah, I hear ya," Jonathan says, high-fiving Devon and Toby.

"Yup," that's all Toby can say.

I shake my head so I can shake away the sound of them. Heather is now looking out the window. I imagine her willing the bus to start rolling and then arriving at my stop instantly, and then I'll be safe.

"Hey, Ratner," Bullock says. He's now standing in the aisle at my seat while other kids push past him. Heather turns away from the window and looks up at him. His wild smile widens when he sees her. He looks at her and then at me. Her and then me. "What's up, Ratner?" He puts out his hand for a high-five. What? I can't tell if he's serious or not.

Whether it's a trap or not. Like an idiot I try to give him a high-five. He swipes his hand away. A trick. He's laughing. "Uuup, too slow, Ratner."

My stomach stirs like it did the last time I was on the bus. The electricity. Like I have an alien in my guts again. It just sleeps there and Robert Bullock pokes him; wakes him up. If I didn't just stop punching him, if someone would have pulled me off like my dad said to wait for, this would be done, over. If I didn't think so much, if my brain would just shut the hell up, I could have just kept punching and punching. If I lived in Las Vegas, right now, I'd be in some Lite-Brite McDonald's chowing on a Big Mac, and all the electricity would be on the outside of the building instead of inside of me.

Bullock sits down right next to me so now I'm in the middle of him and Heather as the bus starts moving. Heather looks out her window again, about to enjoy the scenery or something, almost oblivious to this. I mean, we were really talking before he came on the bus. Nothing can ever just be normal.

"Hey, Heather, you like Ratner's dotted eye?" Bullock says, tapping her shoulder.

"Why don't you make like a tree and leave?" she says.

"Oooh, I'm sorry. I didn't know you guys were boyfriend and girlfriend."

Heather and I respond to this at the same time, "We're not."

She says, "How about you make like an *idiot* and leave?"

The electricity is going crazy in my guts now. It is a monster in there, I know it. A dragon maybe. No, an animal. But it feels like the whole Las Vegas Strip is stuck in there.

Robert laughs at Heather's comments and while he's laughing looks back at Jonathan and Toby who are laughing too. Devon is just smiling like he's telling Robert to get on with it, get the job done.

"See that dotted eye?" Robert says. "Yeah, I gave that to him, Heather."

"Shut up," I say. But I don't know if anybody heard me.

"What?" He flicks my ear. "Speak up, Raaatner. I can't hear you."

"Grow up, Robert," Heather says.

He flicks me. Again. The monster is stretching, yawning, waking up. I see Robert take one step into the aisle and cock his fist. This time he's ready.

I'm up, standing on top of the bus seat. Looking down, again, at this Robert Bullock. I got up here so fast, faster than I am. Because I am not me; it's the animal and electricity that's got me up here, that's got my fist cocked back, that's wiped the smile from Bullock's face, that's—I stop myself. Stop. Stop. Stop!

And I think. Take a breath, un-cock my fist, switch my feet and step back. . .into side stance. I unclench my fists, and bring my arms up, one in front of my face, the other loose by my chest: the same fighting stance I get in when I spar at karate.

This time, I'm going to be in control of myself and my electricity. Breathe in through my nose, out through my mouth – my eyes steel and ice, staring at Robert's. Focused. I don't want to fight Robert Bullock at all, but if I have to, I'm going think. I'm going to be in control.

Because I am not an animal.

And, it ends here.

Robert leans all the way back, loads his right fist behind his ear, and swings it toward me. It's like he's heaving a heavy truck tire my way, only because we never throw right hooks in karate. Why? Because they take an hour to get to the target and you can see them coming from a mile away. Right as I raise my left arm to easily block his punch and strike his face with my right fist, the bus comes to a screeching halt. Since I'm standing on the seat, I go flying into the back of the seat in front of me and to the floor.

Everyone else just kind of topples forward and then collectively topples back into their seats. I see Timothy Chesterfield, who always sits in the front seat, land face-forward into the aisle. He picks up his glasses, and while he fumbles to put them back on, the bus driver picks Timothy up literally off the ground and totally places him back into his seat. Timothy says, "Thank you, sir," as the bus driver walks back to the control panel and pulls a lever and then another one.

I get up off of the floor and sit down in my seat. My heart's racing again, pulsating in my ears.

Heather looks out the window and says, "Oh my God, he stopped the bus in the middle of Kressen Road. Look."

I lean over her and look out the window. Her hair is right by my ears and it smells like pineapples, not watermelon. I was wrong about watermelon, but she is still truly tropical. Why do girls smell like the best fruit all of a sudden? When I look out the window, I can see the big stop sign that extends out of the bus like a giant elbow, and a bunch of cars lined up behind the sign.

The kid behind me says, "I've never seen the bus driver's whole face before."

The kid next to him says, "Just his big eyeballs in the rearview."

Heather looks back and says, "Shhh."

"Good afternoon boys and girls," the bus driver says in that wacky accent. "Welcome to this month's Tattoo Show-N-Tell Installment."

Heather looks at me with a confused expression. I don't know how to explain this to her quietly and quickly before the bus driver arrives at our seats. I say really fast, "Ah, every month, he shows us a tattoo. He's got 10 of them. Ah, I think."

"Now I know it's not Monday, but, well, so what," the bus driver says, walking toward us, breathing extra hard because he's trying to walk and talk at the same time.

"What?" The kid behind me asks. "What's he saying?"

Heather leans in to me and whispers, "He's from Poland."

"Really?" I say.

"Yeah, my great-grandmother is from Poland, and she sounds just like that."

Looking at him up close now, the man must be at least 80 years old, but his arms are huge and still full of muscles. He's not that tall, but he's big, like a bulldog. He unzips his jacket and tosses it backward onto his driver's seat. So he's just a collection of arm muscles that end at those orange Philadelphia Flyers wristbands.

I hear several cars honking their horns, but it doesn't seem to disrupt the bus driver. He ain't budgin' his bus. Heather looks at me and I look at her, and I shrug my shoulders. I take a peek over at Robert, who took the seat across the aisle, and he no longer has that wide-eyed wild grin on his face. He looks scared.

More cars beep. Sounds like those New York City traffic scenes you see in the movies. The bus driver opens the front door and calls out, "Just a minute!" We all nervously laugh at that. He leaves the door open and hobbles back to the front of the bus.

But he keeps walking, slowly down the thin lane that divides the two sides of the bus. "This, boys and girls. . ." He stops right in front of our seat and raises his left arm high in the air so we can see his wrist. After pushing the dirty orange wristband off, he tosses it to Heather who instinctively catches it. His fingers almost touch the ceiling.

"This was my very first tattoo," he says. "I got the other ones thinkin' they might draw attention away from this ugly one. It's just numbers, as you can see. 'Cause there was a time when that's all I was. . . this number."

There is so much beeping outside that it sounds like a pep rally for a high school football game. But no one on the bus is looking out the window.

Since he's right in front of me, I can't help but be fixated on the bus driver's wrist where those black numbers are.

"In 10 or 20 years, I don't know for sure, there will be no survivors left. It will just be *you*."

He points at Robert Bullock. He points at me.

Heather takes my hand in hers and squeezes it.

Mr. Cebulski is right in front of Robert Bullock and me now, and I swear this bulldog of a bus driver drops to his knees and stares dead into my eyes and then Robert's and whispers, "I'm beggin' ya. . .I'm tryin' to drive here."

His arms are outstretched and we can see the numbers. All of them.

CHAPTER FIFTY-FOUR

The next day, I sit in the very back of the bus, the same seat Robert Bullock sat in when I smashed his head against the back window and stopped. My head is up. He climbs the bus steps and I watch him until our eyes meet. I need to see him see me. He does. And then he sits in the middle of the bus with Devon. Not next to me. That's all I know.

I'm drawing three-dimensional boxes on my notebook during English class while my teacher hands back our final compare and contrast paper. We handed it in last week, before all of this, when Sara Rothman was still alive and coming home maybe. Mrs. Grammar Tree is giving one of those speeches about how most of us disappointed her with our efforts on this paper. She's taught us the word "perfunctory" this semester, which pretty much means we've put a combination of no thought and effort into our writing.

I'm sure that my paper will come back with a giant "P" for perfunctory because I didn't really follow the assignment directions. I mean, we spend the whole semester growing these grammar trees, and then all of a sudden we're supposed to compare and contrast something to something else and make it sound good? What? Winter to Fall? Snickers to Milky Ways? The Eagles to a football team that wins? What I did was turned on *Super Friends,* made myself some SpaghettiOs, and wrote what was in my head.

I see Monica Johnson get her paper back and give the nastiest sigh, just like Marna. She quickly shows it to one of her tight-jean-wearing friends, like she can't wait to show off her lousy grade, and whispers, "I got a D, do you believe that? I worked really hard on this too." She slaps the paper upside down on her desk so that the teacher can hear and see her disgust. But this doesn't seem to stop Mrs. Grammar Tree from handing back the rest of the papers while giving what I think is a perfunctory speech about our perfunctory efforts. And with this big build-up of how lousy all the papers are, I'm really nervous about getting mine back.

But she doesn't give mine back. What? I know I handed it in. I didn't re-write it or anything, even after I accidentally splattered some SpaghettiO sauce on it.

Mrs. Grammar Tree walks to the front of the room and turns around to face us with her hands behind her back.

"There were only two As," she says to us as she swings both her arms forward. In each hand is an A paper, I guess. Is one of them mine? That's impossible. "I'd like us to listen to them. If the authors would come up in front of the class and read their essays, the class would be a most gracious audience. First up, Mr. Ratner."

Look, I'm not going to lie, my face is turning hot and red and my heart is doing what a heart does when it's being attacked – it tries to bang itself against my rib cage so it can leave my body.

"Ah, thanks," I say. "But I'm okay."

Everybody is looking at me.

"Excuse me, Mr. Ratner?" Mrs. Grammar Tree says, all teacher-y.

I look at everyone looking at me.

"I don't, I mean, it's okay, I don't need to read it. Thank you. Ah. For the A."

The class starts to snicker, but Mrs. Grammar Tree sticks out her hand like a giant stop sign and gives the obligatory, "Excuse me," to the class. She walks up to me and places my paper on my desk. It's got a shiny A, written in green ink on it. There's a sticker too, a smiley face. Mrs. Grammar Tree wrote in big curvy letters, WOW!

"You could do it, Larry, and people would like it," she whispers in my ear.

I say nothing and she walks back up to the front of the room, slower than her usual walk. Like she's stepping on a collection of semicolon stones on her way.

But then I think of Sara and her letter to me. The real one. I have this vision, or maybe it's a wish: a wish-vision. It's me sitting next to Sara in *this* English class, and we've been talking *all* year. And when Mrs. Grammar Tree waddles away, Sara blows her bangs off of her forehead like she does, nudges me with her elbow, and smiles.

"Our second A writer—" Mrs. Grammar Tree starts to announce.

"Okay," I interrupt her. Which violates classroom rule No. 12.

"Excuse me, Mr. Ratner?"

"I'll, I'll read it," I say.

Mrs. Grammar Tree smiles too, but not too big. She's generally not a happy person at the workplace. But today she smiles at me. "Very good then. C'mon."

I walk up and stand where in a million years I would never want to stand. Sweat drips down my forehead, and I swear the piece of chipped tile I'm standing on will give way any second and I will fall into a dark pool full of hungry sharks. It could happen.

She nods for me to begin. I don't. I'm sort of frozen. She leans down and whispers to me again, "Just read and it will be wonderful."

I look first at the audience. They are looking at me, which I hate, and I can't help but look at them too. Then I'm staring at the tile floor. My heart is thrashing and thumping, beating hard in my ear drums. Mrs. Grammar Tree has her hands together like she's either going to clap for me or pray for me. I finally lift my head, and then I say something out loud, "For my *friend*, Sara."

I realize, too, that the paper in my hands is also the best friend I've ever had in my life. I hold it tight and, well, I just read:

A BRAND NEW HERO

It used to be that I would wake up early just to watch the Justice League on Saturday mornings. I loved watching the heroes of the Justice League fight evil. But then I got a newspaper route and had to wake up early all of the time.

Today I delivered my newspapers for the last time. Yeah, I got fired, from a job I didn't want anymore. I apologized to my boss at the paper route and he was cool about it, but he said certain actions have irreversible consequences. That's how he said it too. Just like my mom does. He thanked me for my honesty, but said after I deliver the papers today, there would be somebody new delivering the next day. He has never fired anybody for throwing newspapers off of a roof before. He said that was classic, but that I was still fired.

The class, the audience, is laughing. I look up, surprised. I almost smile. Wait, inside, I am smiling. My voice isn't as shaky when I start reading again.

It's only fair. People want their news. Sometimes I turn to the world news page and think about other places in the world where kids my age, who could be my friends if I lived there, already know how to use guns. Sometimes I turn to the comics page and think about my superheroes.

*See, the thing is, all superheroes end in MAN. Bat**man**. Super**man**. Aqua**man**. I want to invent a new hero called **Bar Mitzvah Man**.*

More laughs. Which surprises me when I look and read the next words.

I'm serious. Yeah, Bar Mitzvah Man, where he uses his tallis (which is like a shawl Jews wear at temple services) as a cape and his yarmulke as a boomerang type of Frisbee weapon.

More laughs. And some kid shouts out, "That'd be cool," and another kid shouts out, "And instead of bullets, he could have Hanukah candles in his holster that are like fire arrows that never flame out."

"Shhh, shh," Mrs. Grammar Tree says, smiling. She seems to like the enthusiasm in the room, but she wants me to keep reading. "Larry, go on."

And somebody else says, "Yeah, keep going."

So, I do:

Bar Mitzvah Man lives in Poland, like Poland is Metropolis you know, and he breaks through the ghetto walls and he catches bullets before they go into peoples' heads. And he can go into concentration camps and beat up the SS men and save peoples' teeth caps from being removed and their skin from being made into soap.

But the thing is, Bar Mitzvah Man could never really stop terrorized concentration camp victims from throwing themselves on electric fences, you know? I mean maybe he could stop a few, but surely there will be someone else that he's just not in time for. Or an SS guy who decides which line you go into; the line that goes to the work camp, or the line where everyone gets shot to death. How can Bar Mitzvah Man, as great as he is, know which line to save? I mean, he can't read minds – that's just not one of his powers.

This is what I mean. Maybe I'd rather be Aquaman and just swim under the water where you can't hear any of it.

*Maybe that's why all these superheroes, these super **men**, are so lonely. As good as they are, superheroes know they can't stop it all. For every one person they save, another person is throwing himself on the electric fence. Or, even, being in the wrong place when the other side of the wall retaliates. Even by accident. This has to drive Bar Mitzvah Man crazy, like it haunts him.*

Sometimes during my paper route I go to the roof of the apartment building and watch the sky and I think about what if these newspapers were magic, you know. Part of me wants to step on one and ride it like a magic carpet to Las Vegas. Take a ride down the Strip where all the magic lights will make me grow and shine. And start all over again.

Part of me wants to become the tattoo on my bus driver's arm and come to life. Aquaman. Then I'll dive off the top of the apartment building. . .right into the great wide ocean and hear nothing but water. And see my friends. All the different colors, sizes and shapes. Maybe grab hold of two dolphins, close my eyes, and take a ride. . .

When I finish and look up, there's silence. Monica Johnson is staring at me, her mouth sort of open. Actually, so is the whole class. Mrs. Grammar Tree starts to clap and everyone else is clapping for me.

More clapping.

Mrs. Grammar Tree says, "Wow" out loud and then whispers, "See?" into my ear as some of the class actually stands and continues to clap.

For the first time in my entire life of being a short person, I don't mind everyone looking at me.

CHAPTER FIFTY-FIVE

The bell rings. Bells always ring, and they always end things. Sometimes being saved by the bell is not really true.

I'm walking tall. Toward the bus. My last week on that thing and I can manage it. I'm a tall kid all of a sudden; I may have to duck going up the stairs.

"Larry?!"

I turn. It's Monica Johnson, and she's trying to run toward me but her tight jeans won't let her get into a full stride.

I haven't talked to Monica Johnson since, like a total fool, I asked her to square dance.

"Wait," she says.

I wait. Because she's beautiful and she told me to and I haven't yet figured out how to be all the way rude to people I should be all the way rude to.

"That, that was amazing," she says, all out of breath.

"Thanks," I say, turning to leave.

"I really like what you said about being under water, you know, where you can't hear all the noise, you know. I mean I never thought of it that way, but it makes so much sense 'cause when you come up for air—"

"Sorry," I say, interrupting, "but I gotta catch this bus." I don't want to listen to her, and I don't want to miss my ride home just because Monica is still totally hot.

"Oh," she says, deflated. "Yeah. Sorry."

I start to walk away. So weird. Monica Johnson. Weird.

"Hey," she calls after me. I turn around again. "Maybe we could go roller skating or something. Or talk on the phone or whatever, maybe."

I walk back to her, up close now 'cause I want to.

"Monica, we're moving. Me and my family."

"What? You're moving? I never heard that."

I smile, glance at my bus to make sure I don't miss it. Kids are still piling on, so I can do this right here. "To Israel," I lie.

"Israel?" She can't believe it.

"Yup." I smile.

"Wow."

"Someday, I'm gonna be in the army." I back away toward my bus and leave Monica standing by herself. . .stuck. It's kind of a cool view.

TATTOO SHOW-N-TELL #10. . .
FINAL INSTALLMENT

*O*n my chest here. Take a look. Right over my heart are these two Hebrew letters: חי. It's what my Jewish friends call a CHAI. Means LIFE.

I try not to take mine too seriously, eh.

So I can live it right.

Okay, then.

Sit back. . . and enjoy the ride.

Here we go.

ACKNOWLEDGEMENTS

If you were my student in ENGL 3310, 7735 (writing methods) and/or ENED 4414 (teaching English methods) at Kennesaw State University between 2004 and 2015, your prints are all over this manuscript in some form or fashion. Saying thank you is silly; it's like chewing on popcorn and trying to blow a bubble. Simply, there is no book without you. In an effort to embrace best practices, I wrote alongside you, and together, we made each other write real and from the heart, just like Tom Romano and the late G. Lynn Nelson taught us to do. Many of you are now teachers in middle or high schools, writing alongside your students - giving to them the way you gave to me when I shared early short pieces and full drafts of this book, and you helped me make it better. Again, there is no book without you.

A special thanks to the late G. Lynn Nelson for your mentorship in Writing and Being. Without your short prompts that kept sending me back to my 13-year old self with my students, there'd be no book. More than that, you've taught me a ton about teaching and the power of story. And mostly, I just miss you.

When you try to teach yourself how to write a novel, it ends up taking a long time, an embarrassingly long time. So along the way, there were so many people who directly and indirectly helped me. First, I want to thank my agent, Susan Schulman, for believing in my talent and ability. I also want to thank all the fine folks at GoodReadsPress. Much appreciation goes to David Groff for your editorial work on this book. Your belief in Larry and his journey, along with our impromptu discussions over the phone about the publishing industry, talking me off the edge so to speak, were invaluable. I hope to work with you on future projects. Thanks to editor Laura Backes Bard for your great work on an earlier draft. A special huge thanks to copy editor/proof reader Julie Lindy. Your authentic love for my book, made getting meticulous (and always right) edits feel like the ideal collaboration between editor and author. You are tops, and I think every author should seek you out before submitting their final draft.

A special shout-out to Darren Crovitz, Jennifer Dail, Michelle Devereaux, Michelle Goodsite, Rob Montgomery, Ryan Rish, Katie Mason, Carol Harrell, Jim Cope, Dawn Kirby, and Sarah Robbins - my past and present English Education colleagues at KSU - for your support of my writing and teaching, and my inappropriate humor. Your support and acceptance of me, my unique spot in our program, means the world to me. Ditto to our department chair, Bill Rice, who was always supportive of my writing, and was truly understanding of how hard it is to write a novel and get it published.

Thank you to my ASU English Education mentors Allen Pace Nilsen and James Blasingame. You both (re)introduced me to young adult fiction in such a way that swept me off my writer feet. I hope you know how influential you've been for me. Your prints are all over this book too.

Thanks to Tony Grooms for reading a later draft of this novel, but also for your mentorship. Thanks too to Jenny Sadre-Orafai for your big-time support as a writer and a friend.

Ron Carlson, Jim Leonard, and Steven Dietz, you are amazing writing mentors, and I am forever grateful to you.

Thank you to Sandy Davis and her 8th grade ELA teacher colleagues at Simpson Middle School for piloting this book with their ENTIRE 8th GRADE in Spring of 2016, and then being the first school to adopt *BLOOD* into their yearly ELA curriculum. Teachers like Sandy and schools like Simpson MS make it possible for new YA fiction to live and thrive IN the classroom. Bravo!

Thanks to Jennifer Simmons, Ben Simmons, and Heather Braun for also read- ing earlier versions of the book and giving great feedback.

Thank you tons to my in-laws Vivian Tannenbaum and Nick Pocock and Phil Tannenbaum for always believing in my writing and writing career.

To Holden and Rebecca Levy, the teenagers who live in our house and eat our food, thank you for saying you liked this book even though there are no wizards or zombies in it, and it probably made you think about things you'd rather not think about. But mostly, I hope I made you proud. Thank you to Simeon Levy for liking my book even though you don't know how to read yet. And thank you most of all to my ideal reader: Libby. Thank you for being the ideal mom too, holding our family up and together and healthy, so I can attempt to imagine stories. You are the real hero of this one.

Thanks to my older sister, Maris, especially for your friendship. It's invaluable to me, sometimes the only lifeline I have.

Finally, I dedicate this book to my parents, Thelma and Jay Levy, who always did their best for our family, and their best was more than enough, even when I didn't know it.

About Aaron Levy

A former high school English teacher, Aaron Levy served as an Associate Professor of Creative Writing and English Education at Kennesaw State University in Atlanta, GA. In the summer of 2016, however, he began working full-time as the Director of Academics for the **Georgia Film Academy**.

He earned an MFA in creative writing and a PhD in curriculum and instruction from Arizona State University – go Sun Devils! His first work for young adults, *Pizza With Shrimp On Top* (Dramatic Publishing), has enjoyed over 60 national and international play productions, and was nominated for the 2007 Distinguished National Play Award for the Middle and Secondary School Audiences. Recently, his stories have appeared in *Bohemia Art & Literary Journal*, *Every Day Fiction*, *Black Heart Magazine*, *Linguistic Erosion*, and *Eleveneleven Arts and Literary Journal*.

In his free time, and when he's not injured, Levy loves to ~~play~~ attempt basketball…and plays high above the rim! *Blood Don't Lie* is his debut novel.

For more information about Aaron Levy and his work, along with tons of teacher resources for *Blood Don't Lie*, visit **www.aaronlevy.org**.